CHOSEN BY THE FIRE DRAGON GUARD

ARIA WINTER

JADE WALTZ

Purple Fall
Publishing

Published in the United States by Purple Fall Publishing. Purple Fall Publishing and the Purple Fall Publishing Logos are trademarks and/or registered trademarks of Purple Fall Publishing LLC.

Cover Design: Kim Cunningham of Atlantis Book Design

PRINTED IN THE UNITED STATES OF AMERICA

Dedication

To my husband: Thank you for all your love and support. You are not just my husband, you are my best friend and my rock. I love you more than anything.

-Aria Winter

To My Husband,
Thank you for being my support and rock during this writing journey. I love you!

-Jade Waltz

CHAPTER 1

HOLLY

I've never been particularly brave. When we set out on the colony ships, I was only a child. I remember staring out the window as we took off from Earth. At first, fire enveloped us as we broke through the atmosphere, then there was nothing but the dark void of space punctuated by billions of bright points of light.

My younger sister and I were completely and utterly captivated with our family's *new adventure*, as my parents called it.

Our adventure turned out to be harder than we'd anticipated. My father died in an accident, leaving my mother to raise me and my sister all by herself; I know it was difficult for her.

The day pirates attacked our ships we were separated. Everything happened so fast; it was complete and utter chaos. An explosion rocked the ship and sent me flying across the hallway. The last thing I remember is the sharp *crack* of my ribs breaking as I slammed against a metal panel and everything went dark.

I woke up to find we'd crashed on an alien world full of dragon shifters. The Drakarians are good people, for the most part. At first, I was afraid when I saw them in their *draka* forms when they came to get us from the desert.

In *draka* form, they look just like the ancient dragons portrayed in old Earth myths. But when they shifted into their two-legged state, and I saw how much Lilly trusted their leader—Prince Varus of the Fire Clan—I was no longer so afraid. Ever since then, they've given us food and shelter and done everything they can to welcome us into their society. We're fortunate they found us and decided to take us in after we crashed on their planet.

It's just that everything here is so new and different. Each day presents new challenges of its own. I want to be brave as I plot a course for my future, but it's hard. I've always had my mother and sister. Now that they're gone, I still feel so lost. Every day I send a silent prayer to whomever may be listening, to please keep them safe and help us find them—wherever they are.

The sun is just barely peaking over the horizon as I walk through the Fire Clan castle's palace gardens, enjoying all the beautiful flowers and lovely green foliage. It's so strange to find an oasis of lush greenery in the desert. Long vines drape over the walls, dotted with tiny, glowing blue flowers. They sway in the dry, desert breeze like living curtains. Pebbles crunch beneath my feet as I follow the path toward the large fountain in the center. Streams wind throughout the space, providing natural irrigation to the many flowering bushes with vibrant purple, yellow, and red flowers.

It's so peaceful and meditative here. I love having my tea and breakfast in this spot before I begin the rest of my day. The gardens are the best perk of living here in the palace.

The soft crunch of pebbles behind me, draws my attention and I turn to find Rakan. He gives me a warm smile. "Good morning, Holly," his deep voice rumbles above me.

Heat flushes my cheeks as his intense gaze holds mine. "Good morning, Rakan."

"May I join you?"

Nervous, I nod. He sits down on the bench beside me, and I get butterflies in my stomach when he smiles at me again. Rakan is so handsome, I can't help but get nervous around him.

He's tall with broad shoulders, a body made of hard planes of rippling muscle, and a long, tapered tail. His scales and wings are a gorgeous shade of orange-red that compliments his crimson eyes. Black horns sweep up from his head, making him appear even taller. With a strong jaw and regal nose, he's a gorgeous man by any definition.

I've practically been in love with him since he flew me on his back out of the desert. It hasn't even been six months, but it feels like so long ago since his people brought us to their city from our crash site.

As the personal guard of Prince Varus of the Fire Clan, he's one of the strongest warriors among their people. We're just friends, but I wish so much that we could be more to each other. But I doubt he'd ever want me.

I'm not brave, fierce, or even particularly strong. I'm the opposite of Drakarian women, who are not only larger than the men but also lethal warriors.

"I brought you something for first meal," he says, and I smile as he holds out a plate with fresh fruit and bread.

He's so thoughtful.

"Thank you, Rakan. You don't have to bring me food every morning. I know you have things to do and—"

"It is no hardship," he interrupts. "I am glad to do it."

I smile. "Thanks."

My gaze darts briefly to his chest. I keep hoping that the glowing fate mark will appear there for me, but it hasn't. If it did, maybe he'd want to be more than just friends.

Some of my friends are already married to Drakarian men, and a few are even expecting. They aren't just married; they're fated to these guys. A glowing mark appears on a Drakarian's chest when they find their fated mate.

Most times, the mark glows upon first sight, but sometimes it can take a while to appear.

I'm hoping that's the case with Rakan. With a wistful sigh, I think on how wonderful it would be if this happened because when he smiles at me as he does now, I dream of what it would be like if I were his and he were mine.

I guess I'm lucky, in a way, that he's not really interested in me. Without the glowing fate mark, I'd never feel secure dating him anyway. There's always the risk he might be fated to someone else and then I'd get left behind with a broken heart.

His red eyes search mine. Their vertically slit pupils contract then expand as he stares down at me. "There is something I have been meaning to ask you."

"What is it?" I ask, and then take a sip of my tea.

"I wish to know about human courtship and mating rituals."

I blow out my drink, coughing and sputtering into my cup.

His eyes widen. "Are you all right?"

My cheeks heat in embarrassment as I cough again to clear my throat, barely managing to nod. "What exactly do you want to know about it?" I ask a bit hesitantly.

"How to entice a human female to become my mate."

Unbidden jealousy fills me. I wonder who he's got his eye on. "You... uh... have someone in particular that you're thinking of?"

He dips his chin in a firm nod.

My gaze goes to his chest again. "What about the fated mark?" I ask. "You're not going to wait and see if it happens for you?"

His red eyes meet mine evenly. "I believe in making my own fate. That is why I ask for your help in learning how to properly court and mate a human female."

I ask the most obvious question. "Have you already told her how you feel?"

He shakes his head. "I overheard her say that without the fate mark, she does not wish to chance bonding to a Drakarian male. So now, I must find a way to convince her otherwise."

Well, that certainly doesn't narrow down who he might be talking about. Almost all the woman in my crew feel this way. All the unmarried ones, that is.

"Will you help me?" he asks, his gaze holding mine intently.

I sigh inwardly. I could so easily lose myself in his eyes. I hate that he's asking me, of all people, to help him woo someone else. But, Rakan is my friend and he's been nothing but kind and thoughtful to me ever since he brought me out of the desert. The least I can do is help him in return. "Yes."

A beaming smile curves his mouth, revealing two rows of fangs. I used to think they were scary, when we first met, but now they I find they only add a lethal edge to his handsomeness. I wish he wanted me. Whoever he's after, she's so blessed and she probably doesn't even know it.

Prince Varus calls Rakan over, and he immediately goes to his side.

The Fire Clan Drakarians are varying shades of red and orange. Varus's scales and hair are a deep crimson color, but Rakan's are more or an orange-red that matches his hair as well. A wistful smile crests my lips as I allow my gaze to travel over him. I think his coloring is definitely more vibrant and beautiful than Varus's.

"Holly!" Lilly calls out.

She presses a quick kiss to her mate, Prince Varus. I watch as he places a hand lovingly over her baby bump before she walks over to me. "Your new robes are here."

I allow my gaze to linger on Rakan a moment more before he disappears back into the palace with Prince Varus. I wonder if Lilly might know who it is that he's interested in.

"That was fast," I reply.

"Their technology is amazing, isn't it?" She grins as she holds out the lovely dark-green fabric I picked out only yesterday. "This is a beautiful color," she adds. "I picked out the blue. What do you think?"

She spins in a slow circle, showing off her new robes. The ocean-blue fabric flutters in stunning contrast to her long, red hair and green eyes.

"It's beautiful, Lilly."

"Yours is, too," she replies. "The green complements your blonde hair and your blue eyes."

"Thanks. Do you know if they finished my undergarments, as well?" I ask, noting she hasn't included them. I picked out fabric for them to make me a few extra sets to keep on hand.

The Drakarians don't wear underwear of any sort. The tailor commented that he finds it strange humans wear strips of cloth to cover their chests and pelvic area since their people do not bother with this, but he said it would be no problem to make these items for us.

Her brow furrows. "The tailor said he had a few more things he'd forgotten at his shop. He promised he would return quickly. Let's go check. Surely, he's already come back by now."

"Okay, but first, there's something I need to ask you."

She gives me a curious look. "What is it?"

I dart a glance at our surroundings, making sure no one is nearby to hear what I'm about to say. Satisfied that we're alone, I lean in and lower my voice a bit so as not to be overheard. "Rakan asked me to teach him about human courtship and mating rituals so he can entice a human female to become his mate."

Lilly laughs. "Oh my gosh. Is that really how he said it?"

I'd probably be laughing too if I weren't so jealous of this mystery woman. "Yes. Do you happen to know who he might be talking about?"

Her expression falls. "No. In fact, I thought he was interested in you."

I blink at her, stunned. "Me?" I wish. "We're just friends."

"Oh." She shrugs. "Then, I have no idea *who* it could be."

I sigh heavily. I realize that I could just ask Rakan, but I don't know if I can bear to know the answer. I don't even want to think of him in love with someone else.

When we first met, I thought for sure he wanted me. *I* was the one who was hesitant at that time because everything was so new. But after the Wind Clan's attack on the city, he backed off and we settled into a comfortable friendship.

I follow Lilly back into the palace. Our footsteps echo across the open rotunda as we approach the main entrance. Despite the massive size of the deep-red and orange structure, all the finely carved, dark, wooden furniture with plush oversized cushions and the tapestries along the walls make the space feel cozy and comfortable.

Rakan walks toward us. "Princess, Lilly." He bows before her and then turns to me. "Holly, the tailor left something for you."

My cheeks heat in embarrassment when I notice my orange-red, lacy bra and panties in his hands. He cocks his head to the side, regarding them curiously. "What are these for?"

My mouth drifts open. "They're undergarments."

"Under… garments?"

"You know. A bra and panties."

His brow furrows deeply in confusion, and my blush deepens. His people don't normally wear clothes, and if they do, they stick to simple robes. Drakarians shift easily between their two-legged and *draka* forms, which resemble huge dragons from old Earth stories. Clothing doesn't survive the shift, so they usually walk around completely nude.

At first, I felt awkward surrounded by nudity, but I've since grown accustomed to it. Besides, it's not like we can see anything improper. The men have mating pouches that conceal their *stavs*—as they call them—within their bodies. I've never seen one, but Lilly says they look like human male anatomy but much larger.

"What is a *bra and panties*?" Rakan asks.

Having noticed my flustered expression, Lilly chuckles. She opens her mouth to speak, but Prince Varus calls out to her. "My desert flower, will you join me for tea?"

She beams. "Of course, my love." To me, she comments, "It's a new nickname he's trying out. I think it's kind of cute. Would you like to join us?"

"Thanks, but I think I'll just catch up with you later."

Lilly and Varus are still in the honeymoon phase of their relationship, and sometimes I feel like a third wheel around them.

She joins her husband, leaving me alone with Rakan. He regards me expectantly, and I realize I haven't answered his question yet.

"This"—I point to the bra—"goes around my breasts." His

gaze flits to my chest. "And this"—I gesture to the panties —"covers my pelvis and backside."

His eyes dart to my hips, and he nods. "Your people only remove these things when you bathe or when you are ready to mate. Am I correct?"

"Uh…" His blunt question startles me, and I need a moment to respond. "Yes."

He holds them up, studying the garments intently. His large hands dwarf them as he rubs the fabric between his thumb and forefinger. "This material is soft, like your skin," he murmurs. "Or the petals of the *loeta*."

I would never tell him this, but I chose the orange-red fabric because it reminded me of his scales. As he peruses the material, I imagine his hands moving over my body, slowly removing those undergarments as he watches me.

Desire pools deep inside me at the thought.

His nostrils flare, and his gaze snaps up. His red eyes search mine as his vertically slit pupils contract then expand until only a thin rim of red remains around the edges.

Rakan steps closer. "So, if a human female removes these items in front of a male, does it mean she is willing to mate with him?"

I hesitate, unsure of how to answer. Finally, I settle on, "It *can* mean that. But she must verbally confirm that's what she wants."

He lowers his gaze, seeming contemplative. When his eyes meet mine again, he hands me the underwear. "This makes sense. It is like the mating chase, is it not?"

I've heard of the Drakarian mating chase. A man chases the woman he's interested in, and when he catches her, she either accepts him and they mate, or she rejects him and they go their separate ways.

"Um…" I hedge, not sure the two are equivalent. "Maybe?" My voice squeaks.

He frowns.

"Holly?" I turn to find my friend, Aria, striding across the atrium. "I just came from the Med Center. Healer Ranas said he's ready for you."

"Oh, good," I reply, happy for the interruption to my awkward conversation with Rakan. I turn to Rakan. "I, uh… guess I'll see you around?"

His eyes flash with concern. "Are you feeling unwell?"

"I've had a headache on and off for the past few days. I wanted to see if there is anything he can do to alleviate it."

"Are you experiencing this headache now?"

My thoughts turn to our earlier conversation. Ever since I found out that he's in love with someone else, my head *has* started to hurt again. "Yes."

Without warning, he lifts me into his arms, steps outside, and spreads his wings. I blink, suppressing a yelp. "What are you doing?"

"I am taking you to the Med Center. Now."

Before I can protest, he beats his wings furiously, taking to the sky. My heart hammers as we fly over the city. I wrap my arms tightly around his neck and bury my face in his chest. I never used to be afraid of heights, but ever since the Wind Drakarian took me the day their clan attacked the city, I've been terrified of flying.

"Are you all right?" Rakan's deep voice rumbles above me.

Unable to speak, I nod against his chest.

He carefully tugs me away, but I cling to him. "Don't drop me," I wail.

He immediately tightens his arms around my form. "I vow that I will never drop you, Holly. We have already landed, but do not worry. I will carry you."

I lift my head in surprise. He touched down so gently, I had no idea we were back on solid ground. "It's all right, then. I can walk. I—I thought we were still flying. I didn't even feel you land."

He tips his chin up. "It is no burden to carry you, Holly."

I start to argue, but as soon as we enter through the doors of the Med Center, Healer Ranas rushes toward us. "What is wrong? Is she injured?"

A memory flits through my mind, recalling that Rakan saved me from the Wind *draka* who tried to kidnap me when their Clan attacked the city. I suffered from a head injury that day. I remember Rakan carrying me to the Med Center for treatment. He stayed by my bed almost the entire time I was healing.

"She is complaining of headaches," Rakan says.

Healer Ranas rakes his eyes over me. "How long have you had these headaches?"

"Intermittently for a few days."

He motions to Rakan. "Place her on the bed."

Rakan lays me gently on the medical bed as if I were made of glass. Healer Ranas runs the scanner over my form from head to toe. He studies the display with a frown that worries me.

"What is wrong?" Rakan asks, his concern echoing mine.

"It is strange," he murmurs.

"What is it?" Rakan snaps. "Tell us."

"Nothing appears to be wrong." Healer Ranas eyes me. "Do you have a headache now?"

"A slight one."

"Do you know what triggers them?"

"The last one happened when I was studying the language modules. Before that, it happened when I was reviewing the teaching information."

"Ah," he says, nodding. "Have you considered that stress may be affecting you?"

At first, I want to protest that he's just dismissing my

11

symptoms, but then I recall that I used to get headaches frequently during my years studying to be a teacher on the ship. The doctor there also told me that they were stress-related, and she was right. They stopped shortly after I graduated and settled into my new teaching job.

"You are certain the pain is not related to her previous injury?" Rakan asks, referring to the day he brought me here during the Wind Clan attack.

Healer Ranas shakes his head. "I am certain." He turns his attention back to me. "We have a tea our people use for stress relief. It is safe for human consumption. Would you like to try it?"

"Sure," I reply. "Anything to get rid of these headaches."

He arches a brow. "Perhaps you are trying to learn too much at once."

I understand what he's recommending, but I don't have a choice. If I want to be a teacher on this world, I have to not only learn their teaching methods and educational technology but their language, as well. The Drakarian children cannot be taught how to write their letters in my human language, so I must learn theirs.

He places a hand on my shoulder. "I suggest you try to reduce your workload and lessons. It would also be a good idea to not spend so much time on the learning modules. Staring at the display for too long can affect your eyes and lead to headaches as well."

I nod. "I'll keep that in mind."

CHAPTER 2

RAKAN

Whan Healer Ranas reports that her headaches are the result of stress and not her previous injury, I release the breath I did not realize I'd been holding. My mind drifts back to the two days she spent in the Med Center after the Wind Clan attack. I stayed by her bedside the entire time she was recovering.

The Healers had assured me she would be fine, but I could not bear to leave her side until I knew for certain that she was awake and well.

I failed her the day of the Wind Clan's attack. She was injured when I fought the Wind draka to save her. We slammed into a building during our fighting and a chunk of debris hit her head, rendering her unconscious.

Because of my failure, I dare not directly proclaim my intent toward her for fear of rejection. I am blessed that Holly still even speaks to me after that happened. A Drakarian female would have deemed me unworthy and already told me there was no hope of ever becoming her mate.

So, I have chosen a different path. I will *prove* to her that I am a worthy mate. And I will attempt to woo her by asking her to teach me what is expected of human courtship and mating rituals. If I learn how to do this properly, perhaps she will consider me then.

My relief at Holly's diagnosis is short-lived when Healer Ranas begins to list all the negative ways stress can affect one's health. He gives her *valo* tea and tells her to return in two weeks.

As we exit the building, she turns to me. "Thank you for coming with me, Rakan. It was very nice of you."

She gives me a dazzling smile. She is the most beautiful female I have ever beheld. Her blue eyes stare up at me as I study her lovely face. My gaze travels over her body, noting the sensuous curve of her breasts and the gentle flare of her hips.

She is smaller than a typical Drakarian female, and it calls forth my protective instincts. As we pass a male Drakarian on the walkway, I note how his eyes rake over her form, and I growl low in warning.

He quickly lowers his gaze and continues on his way.

I dip my chin. "Of course, Holly. I am glad you are well."

Does she not realize that I would do anything for her? Ever since the moment I first saw her in the desert, I knew she was meant to be mine. However, I doubt she feels the same way. Especially after I failed to keep her from harm. Varus claims human females are not like ours—that she might forgive my failure if I simply asked—yet I am afraid to do so. I worry she will reject me if I do not somehow prove my worth in other ways and demonstrate that I will never fail her again.

If she were Drakarian, we could simply perform the

mating chase and she could clearly accept or reject me as her mate, but Varus says human females do not share this custom. They must spend time with a male and get to know him before they decide whether they want him or not.

So, I am spending all the time I can spare with Holly, constantly trying to prove my worth to her. Hopefully, she will soon remove her clothing and undergarments, and declare that she wishes to mate me. However, until she does, I will be patient.

I spread my wings and hold out my arms to her. "Shall I fly us back to the castle?"

She shakes her head. "I have to stop by the school. I forgot my tablet there earlier, and I need it to study the language modules tonight."

I wrinkle my brow. "Healer Ranas just told you that your current workload was the cause of your stress. You should rest this evening. Not work harder."

"I don't have a choice, Rakan. I need to learn your language."

"Why? You have a translator chip, do you not?"

"Of course, I do," she huffs exasperatedly. "How else would I be able to understand you? But if I want to teach, I have to learn how to speak and write the Drakarian language. I also need to study the education modules to learn your people's teaching methods—"

"Why do you need to learn all of this?" I frown.

"So that I can get a job as a teacher here."

I cross my arms over my chest. "You should not put so much pressure on yourself to learn everything at once. You heard what Healer Ranas said about the effects of stress."

She sighs. "If I don't push myself, it will take me forever to learn everything I need to teach here. I don't have a choice."

"Is there not some other job you could do that requires less preparation?"

She purses her lips. "Do you like your job?"

"I love it," I reply without hesitation.

She places her hands on her hips. "Then how would you feel if someone suggested that you stop working as a guard?"

"Ah. I believe I understand now. Perhaps you could somehow reduce your workload and your time spent staring at the display for the learning modules."

"How?"

I pause, considering. As soon as the idea enters my mind, I smile. "I could teach you our language so you do not have to stare at the monitor for the learning modules for so many hours."

It is a good plan. If she agrees, I can spend more time with her. Prince Varus and Princess Lilliana spend hours talking sometimes, which almost always leads to her giving him what her people call *kisses*.

My gaze drops to Holly's mouth. I wonder if her lips are as soft as I've imagined.

"You'd do that for me?" she asks, her blue eyes shining with hope.

I would do anything for her. "Yes."

A brilliant smile lights her face, and she wraps her arms around me in a hug. "Thank you, Rakan. You have no idea how much this means to me. When can we start?"

"As soon as you wish."

When she pulls back, I already miss her warmth in my arms. I am desperate to hold her again. "Shall I fly us back to the castle?"

She considers for a moment then nods. "Sure. I trust you not to drop me." She smiles. "I'll just bring my tablet home tomorrow when I leave school."

With difficulty, I manage to suppress the pleased purr

that threatens to rise in my throat as she steps into the waiting circle of my arms, and I lift her against my chest. I am glad she trusts me to keep her safe while flying.

Perhaps all hope is not lost. If she trusts that I would never let her fall, then some day, she may trust me with her heart.

CHAPTER 3

HOLLY

When Rakan takes me back to the castle, he walks with me to the guest wing and bids me goodnight.

I'm wide awake, however, and eager to get started on our language lessons. As he turns to leave, I touch his forearm. "Wait."

He spins to face me. "What is it?"

Under the scrutiny of his red eyes, I nervously tuck a stray tendril of hair behind my ear. "I... was hoping we could start our lessons this evening."

"Of course." He smiles. "Where would you like to do this?"

I half expected him to protest and am pleasantly surprised he did not. I return his smile. "How about the palace gardens?"

He nods, and we stroll back down the hallway and into the gardens.

Walking down one of many pathways in the garden, I trail my fingers over one of the delicate glowing blue flowers along the wall, and I realize I don't even know where to begin. A disturbing thought occurs to me, and I consider that this might not work. I turn to him. "How can we practice speaking to each other in your language when my translator will just translate it all for me?"

He reaches for the translator chip behind my left ear but stops just short of touching me. "May I?" he asks.

I nod.

The tips of his fingers trace lightly across the skin just behind my ear as he carefully feels for the translator. A small shiver of pleasure runs through me at the contact. My heart rate quickens as his red eyes meet mine. "When I tap your translator, it will disable. You must tap it twice to reactivate it."

Unable to speak, I nod.

He taps the metal, and when he opens his mouth again, a series of guttural sounds leave his mouth. I only understand about a third of his words.

"Can you repeat that?" I ask, clearly enunciating each word to make sure I pronounce it correctly.

He nods and begins to speak again. "Can you understand me when I talk slowly?"

I smile when I catch every word. "Yes."

We sit on one of the nearby carved wooden benches. The moon is barely a sliver overhead, but the glow of blue flowers in the hanging garden vines casts enough illumination that I'm able to make out Rakan's features.

I try to think of something to ask him so we can converse. After careful consideration, I return to our conversation earlier and ask, "Why did you become a guard?"

"My father was a royal guard. I wanted to be just like him when I grew up." A wistful smile crests his lips. "My mother was a fierce and powerful female. Father often told me that the only reason she chose him was because of his work. I knew that if I wanted a strong female to choose me some day, I must prove my strength and courage as a warrior." He tips his chin up with pride. "I was the youngest male ever to be chosen as personal guard to the royal family."

My heart sinks. He wants a brave, strong woman for his mate—two virtues I lack, especially compared to a Drakarian woman. Rakan's people have commented many times on our lack of natural defenses. We don't have claws, fangs, wings, or scales, and I suspect they deem us pitiful. So, I know he'd never want me. Drakarian men desire strong women, not weak ones.

"What about you?" he asks, pulling me back from my thoughts. "Why did you become a teacher?"

I should have realized he would ask this question. It's only natural, given what I just asked him. I close my eyes briefly as painful memories surface in my mind.

"Because of my dad," I explain. "He died when I was a child." A tear slips down my cheek, but I quickly brush it away.

Rakan's shoulders slump. "My father died as well, protecting Varus's father during battle. It is a terrible tragedy to lose a parent. My heart grieves with yours."

Emotions lodge in my throat, but I manage to speak around them. "My heart grieves with yours, as well."

He nods solemnly, and I continue, "When a sickness swept through our ships, so many children were orphaned because their parents fell ill. I remembered the pain of losing my dad, and I... wanted to do whatever I could to help those kids feel less lost. I helped them find other families to stay with, and if no one was available, I'd take them in until I could find them a permanent home."

"That was very kind of you," he comments. "You have a good heart."

I'm not sure how to respond to his statement—I've never

been comfortable with praise—so I simply nod. "A mother in of the families I placed a child with, she was a teacher on one of the other colony ships. She's the one who told me I was good with kids and suggested I look into teaching." I shrug. "So, I did, and I fell in love with it. It's not so much a job as a passion."

His brow furrows. "This is why you work so hard now, is it not? Because you wish to do what you love."

"Yes. My younger sister, Elora, was studying to become teacher as well."

"What happened to her?"

I blink back tears. "We got separated during the pirate attack. She and my mom… I have to believe that they're still out there somewhere, waiting for us to find them."

His red eyes meet mine. "Our people are searching for yours even now."

"I know," I reply. "That's what gives me hope. It's what allows me to focus on my future."

His lips curl up in a faint smile. "I vow to do whatever I can to assist your studies. We will converse every night to improve your language skills, and tomorrow, we will begin writing as well."

I smile. "I'd love that. Thank you, Rakan."

"You are very strong, Holly."

His statement stuns me. I have never thought of myself in this way.

Laughter draws my attention off to the side and I watch as Prince Varus gathers Lilly in his arms and then kisses her long and deep. He places his open palm lovingly on her slight baby bump.

They're so in love. Lilly is so blessed to have such a wonderful mate who completely and utterly adores her.

I look away, feeling as if I'm intruding on a private

moment and notice Rakan staring at me with a look I cannot quite discern.

He quickly averts his gaze. "Will you teach me how to court a human female?"

My heart sinks as his words remind me that he's in love with someone else. Despite my sadness, I reply. "Yes. What would you like to know?"

CHAPTER 4

RAKAN

Her question is the opening I had hoped for. "Tell me what you would expect a male to do when he is courting you."

She furrows her brow as she considers a moment before replying. "I'd want him to spend time with me... getting to know me."

We are already doing this. I am glad we will be able to spend even more time together as I teach her our language. "What else?" I ask.

"Flowers would be nice."

"Flowers?"

She smiles. "When a man is interested in a woman, he gives her little gifts sometimes. Flowers, snacks, jewelry. Things like that."

I file this information away for the future. I will be sure to bring her flowers tomorrow when I meet her in the palace gardens in the morning. Ever since I discovered that she has her morning tea near the fountain, I make sure to go there as well so that I may spend time with her. I also bring her food since I notice that she does not partake of breakfast otherwise.

I tip my head to the side, considering. "Does fruit and bread count as snacks?" I ask, thinking of the items I normally bring to her each morning.

"Yes," she replies. "They do."

I smile. This is good. I am already doing some of the things expected in the Terran courtship ritual. I simply need to incorporate a few more.

As we continue to talk, I subconsciously move my tail closer and closer to her. The urge to wrap it around her ankle and lower leg is difficult to suppress. Males of my kind do this when we are attracted to a female. If a Drakarian female accepts this small touch, it means she is receptive to considering the male as a potential mate.

Holly and I converse for a few more hours before she begins to tire. She yawns, and her eyes grow heavy-lidded. "I think I should probably go to bed," she says.

"I will walk you to your room."

When we reach her door, I watch her disappear inside. The pull I feel to her is so strong, I am reluctant to leave her. I glance down at my chest, wondering if the fate mark will begin to glow across the scales over my hearts.

I wait a few moments, hoping it will appear, but it does not. With a heavy sigh, I continue down the hallway and enter my chambers. I head straight for my bed and drop onto the comforter. Staring up at the ceiling, I cannot stop picturing Holly. Even if my fate mark never appears for her, I would still wish her to be mine.

She is intelligent, thoughtful, kind, and the most beautiful female I have ever seen. I did not know that her father had died. Learning how bravely she carried on after his death, and how she turned her grief into an impulse to help others speaks to her admirable strength of will.

Even now that her younger sister and mother are missing only confirms what I suspected all along: Holly is a strong female.

I wonder now if I could ever truly be worthy of such a powerful female. I do not know, but I must try. I am not yet willing to surrender.

After witnessing Prince Varus and his human mate, Princess Lilly, in the gardens, it only strengthens my conviction.

Varus told me he knew the moment he saw Lilly that she was meant to be his. He knew she was his fated one—his *Linaya*. I understand now what he experienced, because I feel it too.

Holly is my Linaya; she should be mine. I feel it in my hearts... even if fate has not willed it yet.

CHAPTER 5

HOLLY

When I wake in the morning, soft light filters in through the thin red curtains. I allow my gaze to drift around the room. These chambers are luxurious compared to my cabin on the colony ships, and I can hardly believe how fortunate we are to live in such comfort.

Tapestries decorate the red-orange brick walls, depicting scenes of Drakarians in their *draka* form fighting great battles. A fireplace sits on the corner near my king-size floating bed. A floating table and chair adorn the other corner. Directly across from me is a spacious balcony that overlooks the city.

I climb out of bed and step outside to greet the early morning sunrise.

I survey the city. The palace and this district sit above the rest of Valoria. Buildings and houses, shaped from earthen brown-and-red clay, stand proudly atop the mesa. The style is simple yet elegant in design, echoing the castle.

According to Lilly, the wealthier citizens make their homes near the palace, whereas the remainder of the Fire Clan lives in the valley below, along the river that curves around the base of the mesa.

From here, I can see the verdant fields of rich farmlands, fed from the water's canals. Across the river lies a steep plateau. The vivid orange-and-crimson layers of rock are beautiful to behold during the day when the sun hits them just right.

Sometimes I worry that this is all a fever dream. That our new life is all a lie, and I'll wake up back on the ship. I wonder when this fear will dissipate. I love it here; this planet is more beautiful than I could have ever imagined. It's a luxury to wake each morning to the light of an actual sun.

I dress then make my way down to the palace gardens to have my morning tea. It's early enough that most of the palace is still asleep, so I decide to indulge in my guilty pleasure. I slip off my shoes and step onto the lush, green grass.

The earth is soft beneath my feet. So soft, in fact, that I decide to lie down. Closing my eyes, I enjoy the warmth of the morning sun on my skin as I spread my arms wide.

A shadow falls over me, and my eyes snap open to find two red irises peering down in concern. "Are you all right?" Rakan asks.

I jerk upright, smoothing a hand over my long blonde hair. My cheeks heat with embarrassment at being discovered. "Yes," I blurt. "I was just enjoying the morning."

He sits beside me and gives me a handful of flowers. They look like roses but the petals are various shades of green. "These are for you."

"They're lovely." I bring them to my nose, inhaling deeply of the delicate fragrance. "Where did you get these? I've never noticed them here in the gardens."

"I grow them on my balcony."

I smile. "I love them."

His eyes widen. "You love me?"

My head jerks back. "What?"

He blinks, dumbstruck. "You just said that you love me, Holly. Is this truth?"

I stop just short of facepalming myself as more heat flares across my face. I reach behind my ear and tap my translator to reactive it with a nervous smile. "I'm sorry, Rakan. I still had my translator off. This is exactly why I need your help with Drakarian; I'm worried if I don't learn it properly, I'll cause misunderstandings."

He lowers his gaze, a deep frown marring his face. "Yes, I can see that would be a problem for you."

Before I can respond, Lilly and Varus stride through the doors into the garden. "Good morning," Lilly greets brightly. "You two are up early."

I stand, brushing my hands over my robes to remove any dirt, then smile. "Yeah, I thought I'd have some tea before I head to the school."

"Would you like to join us for breakfast?" Varus asks.

"Thank you, but I need to go. I have a long day ahead of me."

"What are you going to do today?" Lilly asks.

A grin of pure anticipation lights my face. "I get to shadow one of the teachers and actually start working with the kids today."

Lilly beams. "That's wonderful, Holly."

"Thanks."

Rakan interjects, "Would you like me to fly you to the school?"

I dart a glance at Prince Varus. Rakan is his personal guard, and I don't want to distract him from his duties. "Thank you, but I think I'll just walk."

He dips his chin. "Perhaps we might have midday meal

together? We could eat and practice your language skills at the same time."

I grin. "That would be great."

"I will see you then," he replies.

As I head toward school, I cannot stop smiling. Today, I get to work with the kids for the first time, and I get to have lunch with Rakan. This is going to be a wonderful day.

CHAPTER 6

RAKAN

Although it has only been a few hours since I saw her, I can hardly wait for midday to come around. As soon as Prince Varus and Lilliana retire to their chambers to have lunch on their private balcony, I report to another guard then make my way to the kitchen.

When I offered to have the midday meal with Holly, we did not discuss any specifics, and so I wish to meet her completely prepared. I retrieve a blanket and fill a basket with dried meats and fruit and bread, then take to the air in a hurry.

Lilly and Varus often sit in the gardens during midday meal atop a blanket with a basket of food. She calls it a *picnic*. Varus has shared that Lilly to do this, and I am hoping that Holly feels the same.

As soon as I reach the school, I find her. She is playing *kalto* with the fledglings in the yard. They appear to be no more than six or seven cycles old. As they take turns hitting the ball to each other, I observe her.

Her golden hair is tied in a loose knot at the back of her neck. I note that as she runs around with the children, laughing and playing, they all remain respectful and do not use their wings to gain an unfair advantage over her in this game.

As I watch her, a wistful smile curves my lips. I cannot help but think she would be an excellent mother to our fledglings, if she will have me as her mate. A deep ache forms in the center of my chest. I fear her rejection, and I can hardly bear the thought of her with another male—becoming a mother to fledglings that are not mine.

Holly grabs the ball and runs toward the goal line. The gaggle of children races after her. Because they are Drakarian, they are much faster than she is despite their smaller size. My heart stutters and stops as they lunge for her, tackling her to the ground.

Panic sparks in my chest. I drop the basket and cloth and race toward her, praying she has not been injured by their weight. I pull the fledglings away, and I'm shocked when she smiles up at me, her blue eyes sparkling with joy.

I blink at her. "You are unharmed?"

She laughs as she stands, brushing the dirt from her robes. I note the red flush of her cheeks and the several long tendrils of her golden hair that have come loose from their tie to frame her lovely face. "I'm fine," she says. "We were just playing."

I give each of the children a pointed look. "You must take great care when playing with your instructor. She is human, and you know they are not as strong as our people."

The children lower their gazes.

"We're sorry. We were just having fun," one says, lifting his gaze to Holly. "I apologize, Miss Holly. We do not want to hurt you."

She smiles warmly at him. "You didn't hurt me, Kovan. I'm fine."

He turns to me, and his eyes widen. "You're Rakan," he gasps. "Prince Varus's personal guard."

I nod.

"Will you teach me how to fight?"

I open my mouth to speak but am uncertain of how to respond.

"What about me?" another chimes in.

"And me?" yet another calls.

Having sensed my hesitation, Holly steps between me and the fledglings. "Now, students, Mister Rakan is busy. You should go along and eat your midday meals."

"Yes, Miss Holly," they reply in almost perfect unison.

I turn to Holly. Only now do I notice dirt smudging her chin and her cheek. "You have some dirt on your skin. Allow me to remove it."

She nods, and I carefully reach out and brush the streaks away with the soft pad of my thumb. Her cheeks turns bright red beneath my touch, and I wonder at this reaction.

When I am finished, I gesture toward the basket of food. "I have brought our meal."

"I'm glad you're here," she says. "I'm practically starved."

My expression falls. "Are you not getting enough to eat in the castle? I can speak with the staff—"

She laughs. "I'm not really starved. It's just a human saying for when we're hungry."

"Ah," I reply. "Well, I have brought refreshments for us to enjoy." I gesture back to the cloth and the basket. "Shall we have a picnic?"

"A picnic?" A stunning smile curves her lips. "That sounds wonderful. I've always wanted to have a real picnic."

I frown. "A real picnic?"

She nods. "On the ship, we'd have picnics, but only in the

virtual reality rooms. I've never actually had a real picnic outside before."

I am glad I have observed Varus and Lilliana so closely, for I will do anything to please Holly. Right now, she appears delighted with the idea of this.

I present to her the various dried meats, fruits, and bread I have packed for our meal. I watch her spread *kinril* all over her bread. It is an extremely sweet paste that is only meant to be used sparingly. She brings it to her mouth, and my jaw drops.

She pauses, eyeing me curiously. "What's wrong?"

"That"—I point to the paste—"is excessively sweet. You might become sick if you use too much."

She laughs, and I'm so charmed by the sound I nearly forget my concern.

"That's the same reaction Varus had when he saw Lilly eating this the other day. Drakarians must have vastly different taste buds because to me, this tastes like peanut butter."

"Peanut... butter?"

"A nut spread we used to eat on sandwiches and crackers." She shrugs. "*Kinril* is actually my favorite Drakarian food so far because it reminds me of this."

I store this information away for later use. I will make sure that I acquire several jars as a gift for her.

As we sit together, I notice a few teachers observing us. Following my line of sight, Holly stands and motions for me to follow her. "I'd like to introduce you to my friends."

I arch a brow. "Friends?"

She nods. "The teachers here are great. They've all been such a tremendous help with the teaching modules."

I'm surprised—even more so when we reach them, and they greet her so warmly. After what happened between Sorella and Talia in the Water Clan territory, we'd feared that more female Drakarians would be aggressive toward the human females.

Ever since the Great Plague decimated our homeworld, there are far fewer females than males, and of those who remain, very few are fertile. Many Drakarian females are now aggressively competitive, viewing others as threats rather than friends. Males of my kind have also become more territorial, especially when competing for a mate.

She gestures to the closest female. "This is Lurila. She's the teacher I've been assigned to follow." She then points to a nearby male. "And this is Brodin. He's been helping me with the teaching modules, as well."

I struggle to suppress the growl rumbling my chest as I shift my gaze to the male. His yellow eyes are practically sparkling as he gazes at Holly. He is clearly attracted to her, and I note that his tail is far too close to her ankle for my liking. I narrow my eyes at him, and he quickly retreats.

Several of the fledglings run up to us, their faces full of eager anticipation. "Are you really Rakan? The strong warrior? One asks. "Will you teach us to fight?"

Another child chimes in, eyes shining. "My dad says you're the fiercest, bravest guard ever."

CHAPTER 7

HOLLY

I watch the children all gather around Rakan, their little faces brightening with excitement as they bombard him with questions about his work and plead with him for fighting lessons.

He crouches down and begins to show them a few defense stances. I smile as I watch them eagerly mimic his movements. Before I realize it, they're practically hanging all over him.

I laugh when he pretends to fall to the ground, felled by their fearsome warrior skills. He rolls on the ground, making mock sounds of distress and pretending that they've defeated him before he pushes them away and springs back to his feet in triumph, grinning from ear to ear.

They cheer and then begin to chase him again.

A wistful sigh escapes me. He's so good with kids. He'll make a great father someday. My gaze drifts to the teachers, and I note some are watching him closely—a little too closely for my liking.

Jealousy rears its ugly head as Lurila eyes him appraisingly. She's one of the few unbonded teachers here. She's told me many times that she wants a strong male for her mate. Judging by her expression as she watches Rakan, I surmise that she's found him.

I walk over to him, and take his hand. "All right, children, I think Rakan needs to finish his midday meal so he can return to the castle soon. Isn't that right, Rakan?"

I glance up at him. Gently, he squeezes my hand in return. I notice he makes no move to release it as we walk back to the picnic blanket, and I'm glad. When we reach our food, we both sit and face each other, his hand still in mine.

He lowers his gaze to our joined hands and gently runs the soft pad of his thumb across my skin. His black claws are retracted so as not to accidentally scratch me. "Is this part of our lesson?"

"Our lesson?"

He nods. "About human courtship rituals."

"Oh," I reply, my cheeks heating. "Yes, it is," I lie. "Humans like to hold hands when they are courting."

"Do you?" he asks.

"I… uh… I've never been courted by anyone. But I do think it's a romantic gesture among couples."

He nods, and I notice he still makes no move to release my hand. My heart hammers as his gaze holds mine. It would be so easy to lose myself in his eyes. I wish that I was the one he wanted to court. Instead, I think to myself bitterly, I'm teaching him how to do it so that he can woo someone else.

"It seems you are finding your place here," he says, changing the subject.

"Yes. Everyone has been so friendly and welcoming."

His eyes dart to Bridon in the distance, and he frowns. "Bridon is unbonded."

"Yes. He's single."

His gaze meets mine. "Perhaps it would be best if you spent less time with him."

I can hardly contain a smile at his words. Maybe he's jealous of Bridon like I was when Lurila was ogling him earlier. Hope soars inside me. If he feels possessive of me, then maybe he feels some sort of attraction toward me. I drop my gaze to his chest, praying I'll see the glowing pattern of the fate mark swirling across his scales.

Nothing happens, and my shoulders drop.

He continues. "I believe Bridon may mistake your friendly nature as an indication of interest in him as a potential suitor."

As I survey Rakan's handsome face, I find myself wishing that he would do so, instead. Surely, he knows I'm interested in him.

I lean forward. "I'm friendly with you, but you don't seem to take my friendliness as an advance."

He frowns. "Because I know you. I understand you have a friendly nature."

My heart sinks. His answer tells me that he hasn't even considered more than friendship where I'm concerned. I pull my hand from his and lower my gaze, trying to hide my disappointment.

CHAPTER 8

RAKAN

Her expression falls, and she lowers her gaze, tugging her hand away from mine. I immediately miss the contact of her skin against my own.

"I have upset you," I state, wondering why she appears distraught.

She shakes her head and stands. "No."

I open my mouth to speak but don't get a word in before Lurila approaches. She spreads her wings wide to express her interest in me. She is an attractive female, but she is not the one I want. No one can compare to Holly. No one.

"I will wait at the edge of the city during the full harvest moon," she practically purrs. She turns and glances over her shoulder, arching a seductive brow. "If you are interested, that is."

I will not be meeting her there—not on that night, nor any other, for that matter. The only female I wish to pursue in the mating chase is Holly. I hold Lurila's gaze but say nothing. I give her a low growl of refusal as is the customary response to indicate that I am refusing and not interested in her offer.

She dips her chin in acknowledgement of my refusal and disappears into the school building. When I turn back to Holly, her cheeks have flared a deep red as she packs up our meal and shoves the items back into the basket haphazardly. She pushes the lot into my arms.

"Thank you for the picnic," she says, but her tone suggests anything but gratitude. She spins on her heels. "Have a great rest of your day."

I want to ask her why she is angry, but she's already striding into the building. I bite back a growl when Bridon greets her with a beaming smile as she enters the doorway. Anger and jealousy flood my system as I take to the air and fly back to the castle, resisting the urge to knock Bridon unconscious for even looking at her.

I crack my knuckles. I believe this day is a good day for sparring. Besides, the warriors need to practice.

CHAPTER 9

HOLLY

As Lurila goes over the lesson plans, I struggle to focus. I need to learn this material. I cannot allow my emotions to get the best of me. So what if I might have introduced my secret crush to his future wife this afternoon? Maybe they're meant to be.

When he growled at Lurila, after she offered herself to him, it reminded me of the way Varus growls at Lilly when he kisses her.

Yet, even as I think this, I cannot ignore the heavy ache in my chest. I was sure that Rakan wanted me when he saved me that day the Wind Clan attacked. He stayed by my side all through my recovery. But then... he did nothing more. He didn't make a single move.

I know Drakarians don't waste any time when they're interested in someone. They simply express their interest, and that's that. Just like Lurila did earlier. They perform the mating chase, then the woman chooses whether they bond or not.

So, I've waited. I've waited months for him to indicate that he's interested, but he hasn't. We visited Water Clan territory a few weeks ago for a celebration, and I kept hoping he'd ask me to dance with him, but he didn't. Every other guard did, however, while he simply stood off to the side and watched.

He then left to confirm that my friend Anna and the Earth Clan prince, Kaj, were all right. He returned before everyone else did, which sparked hope in my chest. I thought maybe he'd come back specifically for me. However, when I asked him why he'd come back early, he simply explained he needed to make sure we were prepped to leave as soon as Varus and Lilly returned from Earth Clan territory.

"Look at this," Lurila says. She holds her tablet out to me. I notice Prince Varus making an announcement on the display.

Teachers file into the room. With a flick of her wrist, Lurila projects the image onto a large floating screen before us. Everyone's attention is glued to the display as Varus announces the return of something called the Harvest Games.

We listen carefully as he explains, "Each Clan will offer up its best warriors. A series of games will be held in each territory, beginning here in the Fire Clan lands."

Lilly stands by his side, her hand resting lovingly on her slightly rounded stomach. I sigh. She looks so happy, and they're so blessed to already be expecting a child. My thoughts turn to Rakan, and I inhale sharply when he steps up beside Varus.

Prince Varus takes his wrist and lifts his arm overhead, and the surrounding crowd cheers wildly. "The Fire Clan's finest, including my personal guard, Rakan, will be entering the games," he says.

Lurila and the other unbonded teachers begin making a

low rumbling purr sound in their chests. Their eyes are glued to the screen, and I imagine this is the Drakarian version of lusting after someone. Apparently, when they look at Rakan, they like what they see.

Drawing in a deep breath, I struggle to push down the jealousy that flares deep inside me. I have no claim to him; it's not like he's my boyfriend or mate. We're simply friends, as he confirmed earlier today, much to my disappointment.

Varus continues, "In each territory, a winner will be chosen. The four champions will be given a place on one of our deep-space ships. They will be among those tasked with patrolling our region of space and defending us from any enemies while searching for humans who may still be lost among the stars." My mouth drifts open as he adds, "This is the highest honor a warrior can achieve. Only the strongest and bravest among us are sent into space for this vital duty."

My heart stops. If Rakan wins, that means he'll leave. He'll be sent into space on one of their patrolling ships, and I'll probably never see him again.

Panicked, I turn to Lurila. I've heard about the Drakarian deep-space ships and, if I'm remembering correctly, they are gone from their homeworld for months at a time. "The people who are assigned to the deep-space ships... how long are gone for?"

She cocks her head to the side. "They return every six turns of the moon and remain planetside for one turn before they go back out."

I blink. "Why do they only come home every six months?"

"Bonded pairs usually only mate less than once every six turns of the moon. This schedule allows those assigned to the ships to tend their mates before returning into space so they do not feel neglected."

My brow furrows. I had no idea Drakarians normally only mated every six months. Varus and Lilly can't seem to keep their hands off each other. She even confided in me once that he was insatiable, and she loved it.

I can barely stand the prospect of Rakan winning and disappearing for six months at a time. If we were together, and he only wanted to sleep with me every six months, I'd learn to live with that. What I don't want, however, is for him to be gone from me for so long.

He's known throughout Drakaria as an exceptionally strong warrior. So, whatever these games entail, I'm sure he's bound to win.

Bridon steps forward. "I will be entering my name to participate."

Everyone cheers but me. I can't be happy for him, or anyone, for that matter. My mind is fixed on the fear that I might lose Rakan forever.

Then again, how can I lose something I never really had in the first place? He isn't mine. I sigh heavily. We're just friends.

When I return to the castle, Lilly greets me as soon as I enter.

"Did you watch the news today?"

"Yes."

She smiles. "Isn't it wonderful? We'll get to travel to each of the four territories and visit Skye, Talia, and Anna during the Harvest Games."

I do my best to offer her an enthusiastic smile, but I realize it falls short when her expression twists in concern. "What's wrong?"

"Will all the guards and warriors be participating?" I ask, hoping she'll report that Rakan has somehow changed his mind and will not join, despite what I saw on the screen just a few hours ago.

"Most will," she answers. "Varus says it's a good way to prove themselves to attract potential mates."

My heart clenches as I recall Lurila's offer to Rakan to meet her at the edge of the city during the Harvest Moon. I know exactly what she was referring to; she wants him to pursue her in the mating chase.

Tears sting my eyes, but I blink them back. "Even one of the teachers—Bridon—is going to participate."

She gives me a curious look. "You look upset. Are you interested in this Bridon guy?"

Before I can answer, Rakan appears from seemingly nowhere and bows low before Lilly. He turns to me, his expression unreadable.

"I overheard that Bridon will be participating," he says.

I nod, and his gaze hardens. "I assessed him earlier. He is weak and does not stand a chance."

He turns and starts for the exit.

"Where are you going?" I ask, confused by his swift departure. "I thought we were going to work on my language studies."

He calls over his shoulder, not bothering to turn around, "To spar with my guards. I will return to you in about an hour."

Only now as I watch his retreating form do I realize he's covered in dirt.

"What has he been doing?" I ask Lilly. "He looks like he's been rolling around in the sand all day."

Lilly laughs. "He's been training and sparring with the other guards since lunchtime."

Of course, he has. He wants to win the Harvest Games so he can impress Lurila. Clenching my jaw, I start to excuse myself, but Lilly interrupts me.

"Would you like to have dinner with me and Varus?"

I nod. Anything to take my mind off Rakan.

CHAPTER 10

RAKAN

As I spar with my warriors, my mind is only half-engaged with my movements while the other half mulls over Holly's conversation with Lilliana. Unbidden jealousy stabs at my chest. Is she interested in Bridon as a mate?

The thought burns like bitter acid in my gut. I curl my hands into fists at my side, spin, and kick out at the warrior sparring with me.

My foot makes contact with his chest, and he flies backward.

I *will* win the games. Then Holly will be impressed with my skills as a warrior. I will prove that I am worthy of her, then maybe she will allow me to pursue her in the mating chase. Perhaps she will even remove her clothing and state that she is ready to mate.

If she does, I will not hesitate to claim her as mine. I have already decided... even if the fate mark never appears, I want Holly and no other as my mate.

My chest swells with pride at the thought of such a glorious female choosing me.

Something moves in the corner of my vision, and I turn too late. Tarok's foot hits my face, and I lose my balance, stumbling to the ground.

A terrified cry pierces the air and I look off to the side to see Holly rushing toward me. I hate that she witnessed this. The last thing I want is for her to see me as weak.

I stare up at the sky, mentally chastising myself for my lack of attention during a fight.

Tarok must be preening. Little does he know that if I had not been distracted, he would be the one on the ground, not me.

Holly drops to her knees beside me and takes my hand. She cups my cheek and turns my face toward hers. "Are you all right?"

I blink up at her. Her gorgeous blue eyes search mine with panic evident behind them. I'm so mesmerized by their blue depths that it takes me a moment to respond. "I am well."

Wincing, I sit up.

Her expression darkens. "What were you thinking?"

My head jerks back, surprised by the sudden anger in her tone when only a moment ago she was so concerned. "What do you mean? I was sparring. I must practice if I am going to win the Harvest Games."

She huffs. "Why is it so important to win that you would risk hurting yourself?"

I gape. "To prove myself, of course. Any female will find me worthy if I win such an honorable event."

She stands. Planting her hands on her hips, she glares at me. "Well, it seems like Lurila already wants you. So, you don't need to prove yourself any further."

"Lurila?" I blink, wondering why she is bringing up the teacher. Holly saw me refuse her offer. I did so right in front of her so she'd know I do not desire Lurila as my mate. "You saw my response to her offer."

She rolls her eyes. "Of course, I did. How could I miss it?"

This is good. She witnessed my obvious refusal.

"Then, what is the problem?" Could she be upset because I refused her friend and mentor? My hearts clench. Does she still not realize that I want only her?

She throws her hands in the air and spins on her heels. "I guess there *is* no problem."

I'm confused by her answer. Despite her words, she seems upset about something but I do not know what.

She storms back to the castle, and I jump to my feet, following her. "Holly, wait!"

She stops but does not turn around. "I'm sorry," she mutters.

"For what?"

"My reaction. I… it's not my place to judge what you do, Rakan. I'm sure you'll win the games, and every female in all of Drakaria will be impressed."

Hope flares in my chest. *Every female in Drakaria*—surely she includes herself in this statement. Now, I must win to gain a chance to claim Holly's heart. I will be victorious, and I *will* prove myself a worthy mate in her eyes.

However, I must be sure I did not misunderstand her words. "You truly believe that every female in Drakaria will be impressed if I win?"

"Yes."

I tip my chin up as my chest swells with pride. "Then, that is what I shall do. Of this, I have no doubt."

She purses her lips. "Neither do I."

My hearts soar. She believes in me already. I can hardly

wait for the games. When I win, Holly will allow me to pursue her in the mating chase. I will catch her in the desert sands, and she will fall into my arms and agree to be mine.

Then I will claim her beneath the harvest moon and seal her to me as my mate.

CHAPTER 11

HOLLY

Rakan goes off to bathe while I finish having dinner with Varus and Lilly. A thought suddenly occurs to me and I look to Varus. "Won't you miss having Rakan as your personal guard if he wins the Harvest Games and gets assigned to one of the deep-space ships?"

He nods. "I will. He is one of our best warriors. But I cannot ask him *not* to participate. It is an honor to compete in the games and it is also an excellent way for a Drakarian to prove themselves to a potential mate."

As Varus continues telling us about the games, I can't stop thinking about the fact that Rakan isn't even interested in me anyway. He told me he's got his eye on someone, but did not tell me who. Now, I wonder if he may have completely forgotten about her in favor of Lurila.

Lilly takes my hand, her green eyes meeting mine in concern. "You seem distracted. Are you all right?"

She's always been able to read me so well. I could never

hide anything from her. I sigh. "I think I'm falling in love with a Drakarian. But I don't think he wants me."

Varus's head snaps toward mine. "Who is it?" He clears his throat. "If you do not mind my asking."

I open my mouth to reply, but quickly snap it shut when Rakan enters the room. He dips his chin in greeting. "I am ready whenever you are to begin your lessons."

"What lessons?" Lilly asks.

"Rakan is teaching me the Drakarian language. We practice speaking without the use of the translator chip. He's helping me learn how to read and write it as well."

"That's great," she replies.

She inhales sharply and then places her hand over her stomach.

"What is wrong?" Varus asks, concern etched in his features. "Are you feeling ill?"

"No." She smiles and then takes his hand and places it over her abdomen. "Our baby just moved."

A slow grin curves his mouth and he presses a tender kiss to Lilly's temple.

She's only a few months along in her pregnancy, but Healer Ranas thinks the baby will be born in six months or less. That's why she's already showing as much as she is. So are Skye, Talia and Anna, for that matter. They all got pregnant really quickly after bonding to their Drakarian mates.

I sweep my gaze to Rakan. He watches Varus and Lilly with something akin to longing in his expression.

I sigh in frustration. He's probably thinking of Lurila.

I excuse myself and he does too. Together, we walk back out into the palace gardens.

The cool night breeze makes me shiver slightly and he looks to me in concern. "Perhaps we should remain inside for our lessons."

"Where would you suggest?"

His brow furrows in contemplation before he replies. "We could go to my rooms," he offers. "And I could make us some tea as well."

"All right."

When we reach his rooms, I notice they're right beside Lilly and Varus's. I guess this makes sense since he's Varus's personal guard. When he opens the door and leads me inside, I'm surprised by how large and spacious it is.

A large floating bed sits along the far wall next to a huge fireplace. He has a separate room off to one side with two plush gray sofas and a table and chairs. As he goes to light the hearth, my gaze drifts to his bed.

The thick gray comforter is spread neatly across the top and I wonder what it would be like to lay there, wrapped up in his arms. Warmth fills me at the thought, and I force myself to look away.

His entire space is neat, tidy and organized. When I glance out at his balcony, I notice the many plants he has growing in various decorative pots. It's lovely and looks like his own personal oasis. There are several green roses like the ones he brought me the other day.

As if reading my mind, he steps onto the balcony and picks a few. He brings them back inside and hands them to me. I smile as I lift them to my nose and breathe in their sweet scent.

He motions for me to sit on one of the sofas. "I will make us some tea before we begin," he says.

Before I can tell him not to go to any trouble, he's already left the room.

It doesn't take long for him to return and when he does, he takes a seat beside me.

I turn off my translator and we begin.

CHAPTER 12

RAKAN

I study Holly closely as we converse. I love how expressive she is. When she struggles to find a word, two fine lines form between her brows as she softly bites her lower lip in concentration. When she finally gets it right, her smile is as bright as Drakaria's sun.

"You were wonderful with the children today," she says. "They were so excited that you came to visit the school."

I smile. "They seem to have great respect for you as well."

"I just hope I can pass all my requirements to become a full-fledged teacher. It would be wonderful to be able to do my job again."

"You will, Holly. I have no doubt about this. You are extremely intelligent."

A stunning smile curves her lips. "Thank you, Rakan."

"The fledglings... are they the same age as the children you taught on the ships?"

Her expression falls. "Yes. I..." Her eyes brighten with tears and she looks away.

I take her hand in mine, squeezing it gently. "Forgive me. I did not mean to stir sad memories."

"It's all right," she whispers. "I just… I worry for them, you know. I wonder where they are and if they are well. When the pirates attacked, I got them all safely to the escape pods, but I don't know what happened after that… how many of them made it." She pauses. "After I ushered the last child onto one of the pods, that's when the explosion hit. It threw me against the wall and I blacked out. When I woke up, we had already crashed here."

I stare at her in wonder. She is as brave as she is selfless. How can I ever be worthy of such an exceptional female? Her people may be smaller than ours, but I realize just how strong they are in other ways.

"We are searching for your people, Holly. Our planet is part of an alliance of several worlds known as the Galactic Federation. They have agreed to join us in this search. If your people are out there, we will find them."

A tear slips down her cheek as she stares across at me. "I'm trying hard to be brave and to push forward with my life, but I miss my mom and my sister so much. We were so close, the three of us. Sometimes, I cannot believe that I'm here, starting a new life. And I have moments where I wonder how I am able to go on without them… without knowing that they're all right."

I meet her gaze evenly and take her hand in mine. "You are able to do this because you are brave and you are strong, Holly."

She shakes her head softly. "I'm not brave or strong, Rakan."

I place two fingers up under her chin, tipping her face up to mine. "Yes, you are. Never doubt this, Holly. You are one of the strongest people I have ever met."

Tears brighten her eyes as she gives me a small smile. "Thank you."

As the night wears on, her eyelids grow heavy. She asks for another cup of tea, but when I return, she is fast asleep on the sofa.

I set down her cup and then kneel before her, studying her closely. Long lashes fan over soft pink cheeks, her mouth is partly open in a small, round *o*. She is so beautiful that, for a moment, I have an irrational fear that she may not be real. I worry this is all a dream and that I will wake up and find myself alone.

Carefully, I lift her into my arms and carry her to the bed. I gently lay her down beneath the comforter. I reach down and brush a stray tendril of hair back from her face and then make my way back to the sofa. I settle onto the cushions. I will sleep here tonight so she may be comfortable in the bed.

I listen as the sound of her breathing becomes soft and even. I revel in the knowledge that she trusts me enough not only to come to my apartment, but to allow herself to fall asleep here as well.

After the attack by the Wind Clan, I had worried she might never trust me or any of my kind. But it seems I was wrong, and I am glad.

She is strong, brave, kind and selfless. I would give anything for her to choose me as hers.

As I stare at her sleeping form, across the room, determination fills me anew. I will prove myself to her in both the ways of her people and my own. I will show her that I am a worthy mate—more so than Bridon could ever be.

And after I win the Harvest Games, I will drop to one knee before her and ask her to be mine.

CHAPTER 13

HOLLY

When I wake in the morning, I'm surrounded by a delicious scent—something akin to warm spice and cinnamon. It reminds me so much of Rakan.

I snuggle into the comforter and breathe deep of the wonderful fragrance.

My eyes snap open as myriad images flood my mind of last night. My cheeks flush with warmth. I must have fallen asleep here.

I glance around the room, half expecting to see Rakan somewhere nearby, but he isn't here.

The door opens and he walks in from the hallway, holding a tray with tea and several items of food. He smiles when his eyes meet mine, and walks toward me.

"Good morning, Holly. I have brought you breakfast."

"That was thoughtful of you," I answer. Embarrassment fills me as I sit up in the bed. "I'm sorry I took your bed last night."

"It was no hardship for me."

As I sit up, I notice there is a small vase on the side table with more flowers. I turn to him and he smiles. "I placed those there for you."

"Thank you."

The mattress dips slightly beneath his weight as he sits on the edge. "I must leave. I have many things to attend to this morning. But you are welcome to stay here as long as you wish." He smiles. "And I look forward to meeting with you when you return from the school."

With that he leaves.

I finish my breakfast and when I step out into the hallway, a small gasp draws my attention.

I turn to find Lilly standing nearby. Her eyes shift to the door to Rakan's room and she smiles. "Are you and Rakan—"

"No."

Her expression falls. "Then, why are—"

"I fell asleep last night while we were practicing my language lessons."

"Oh," she says. "Are things… going well, though? Between the two of you?"

I could pretend to not understand what she means, but she's my friend and I don't want to lie to her. "I think so, but I don't know." I pause. "Sometimes, I think he might have feelings for me, but I'm just… not sure."

She nods. "The Drakarians are different from us when it comes to these things. They're usually so forward, but I did overhear Rakan talking with Varus the other day."

Hope sparks in my chest. "What did he say?"

"He was asking advice on courting a human. Varus told him to take things slow and to not be as direct as their people normally are. He advised Rakan to spend time with her and to allow her to make the first move."

I sigh. "He was probably talking about someone else."

"Why do you say this?"

"Because he asked me to teach him how to entice a human female to become his mate. He wouldn't have asked *me* if I was the one he wanted, right?"

She takes my hand. "I don't know, Holly. What I do know is that you are the only woman Rakan spends time with. That has to mean something."

I nod. Maybe she's right. "I have to get to the school. I'll see you later when I get home, all right?"

"Have a good day."

As I make my way to the school, my thoughts keep returning to Rakan. He insists that I'm brave. Little does he know how much I'm not. I'm such a coward when it comes to him. As much as I'm desperate to know how he feels about me, I can't bring myself to just ask him outright.

Drawing in a deep breath, determination fills me anew. I'm going to tell him this evening how I feel. I'm going to lay it all out and see what he says. I can do this. I know I can.

CHAPTER 14

HOLLY

Rakan has been helping me every evening for two weeks with my language studies and I still haven't found a way to muster the courage to just tell him how I feel about him.

"You are progressing well with our language," he says. "I have noticed no mistake in your choice of words yet this evening."

My cheeks heat at the compliment. "Thanks, Rakan. Maybe I'm getting better because I have such a helpful instructor."

A wide grin splits his face. "Perhaps this is truth," he teases. His expression turns serious. "How are you progressing with your teaching modules?"

"I'm doing well. Lurila thinks I'll be ready to lead my own class by next season."

He smiles. "This is excellent news."

"What about you?" I ask. "Are you ready for the Harvest Games?"

His chest puffs out with pride. "Yes. I am fully prepared. I have no doubt I will be victorious."

I force a smile to my face despite my dread. I don't want him to win. I want him to stay here on Drakaria. "That's great, Rakan."

He tips up his chin. "I have perfected a new move to defeat my opponents."

"Oh?" I ask, feigning interest when all I can think is that I hope he'll lose.

"Yes. Allow me to demonstrate."

He stands and offers me his hand. I take it, and he pulls me up from the bench. He moves behind me, and I twist my neck to glance at him. "What are you doing?"

"Once I get behind my opponent like so…" He bands one strong arm across my waist, pinning my arms to my sides in the process. He pulls me to him, my back pressed against his front. My breath hitches as he leans down and whispers in my ear, "I will immobilize them in a defensive hold."

He snakes his other arm around my chest and grips my chin firmly. Molded against him, I'm painfully aware of his solid build, which forms a wall of hard muscle behind me. I inhale deeply, breathing in his masculine scent. Something akin to spice and cinnamon. My heart hammers in my chest as his warm breath skitters across my skin.

"Try to move."

I do as he instructs, but I'm pinned helplessly. "I can't."

"Exactly," he murmurs. "If I catch my opponent like this, they will have no choice but to concede."

He loosens his grip just enough so I can turn and face him. We're so close, there is no space between us. He doesn't let go, and I make no move to push away from him either.

The cool desert breeze blows through the gardens, and my nipples prick against the fabric of my silk robe as heat pools deep inside me. I'm pressed so close to his body, I can feel his hearts pounding beneath his chest against mine. I've never been so aroused in my life.

His nostrils flare, and a growl rumbles his chest. The vibration shoots straight through me, sending ripples of pleasure to my core.

Gently, he skims the tip of his nose along my temple. The gesture is so tender, and I want him so badly. His mouth is so close to mine. I tilt my face up and press my lips to his.

At first, he stills, but when I trace my tongue along the seam of his lips, he opens his mouth and my tongues find his. It's deliciously ridged, stroking against mine. Lilly said that Drakarians don't normally kiss, but what Rakan lacks in experience, he makes up for in passion.

He wraps his arms and wings around me, holding me close as he plunders my mouth. A low moan escapes me as he takes control of the kiss. He swallows the sounds of my passion, leaving me breathless and panting.

He pulls back and his eyes meet mine. "We should stop," he breathes. "If we don't, I will be tempted to claim you."

The blood freezes in my veins. He doesn't want me after all. I push away from him. "I'm sorry. You're right. I shouldn't have kissed you."

His brow furrows. "Holly, I—"

"No. You're right. We should stop before you do anything that—" The words die in my throat. *Anything you'll regret.* I lower my gaze. He doesn't have the fate mark for me. Why would he want to bind himself to me without it? Besides, he wants someone else anyway. "Goodnight, Rakan."

I turn and stride toward the palace.

"Holly, wait!" he calls out, running after me.

I spin to face him. "It's all right, Rakan. Really. I understand. You don't want to go any further, and I don't either."

He blinks slowly. "Holly, I do not understand. I—"

"Rakan!" a guard calls. "Prince Varus is searching for you."

He turns to the man, then back to me. "Holly, we must discuss this. There has been a misunderstanding."

"I know," I tell him. "It's my fault. We're just friends, and I crossed a line. Besides,"—my gaze drops to his chest,—"you don't have the fated mark. So, I guess we're not meant for each other."

He shakes his head. "Holly, I do not care if—"

"Rakan!" the other guard demands.

He clenches his jaw. "We will speak as soon as I am able —agreed?"

I nod even as my cheeks heat with embarrassment. I would rather not discuss this at all. I pushed myself on him, and I shouldn't have. He doesn't want me. He wants someone else.

CHAPTER 15

RAKAN

I watch Holly's retreating form disappear down the hallway to her room. I do not understand why she is so upset. When she kissed me, I thought she wanted me—that she had decided to accept me as a potential suitor. Varus said a kiss was the first thing Lilly gave him before she allowed him to claim her.

Yet now, something has gone terribly wrong, and I do not understand what. My need for her was so great, I suggested we stop. I feared I would push her into something she is not ready for yet. I know human females are not like ours. Varus has told all of us that, when it comes to the humans, we cannot simply express interest, give chase, and mate, then become one forever. He said they need more time to decide.

I merely wanted to give her time to make certain she wants me. I have not even managed to prove myself to her, so I was surprised yet elated when she pressed her lips to mine and gave me her human kisses.

My lips tingle at the memory of her mouth upon mine.

Her taste was exquisite, and I long to run my hands and tongue over every *tarem* of her body. If she will allow me, that is. I thought she might, but now, I am uncertain.

I find Prince Varus in the throne room with Princess Lilliana. She gives him a tender kiss and then smiles warmly at me. "I'll leave so you two can speak."

I turn to Varus. "You requested me, my prince?"

"Yes, Rakan. I wanted to discuss the upcoming Harvest Games." He studies me for a moment. "I do not doubt that you will beat any opponent. You are the best warrior among all the Clans."

My chest swells with pride at his words.

"However, it occurs to me that I will lose you as my personal guard once you win. I wanted to know whom you would recommend among your warriors to replace you when you leave."

"Tarok," I reply without hesitation. "He is the best of all the Fire Clan warriors, my prince."

Varus arches a brow. "After you, of course."

I grin. "Yes, my prince."

Varus sighs. "What about your human—Holly? Is she pleased that you will be competing in the games?"

I lower my gaze. "I am uncertain."

"Oh?"

I sigh. "Human females are impossible to read. I… thought she wanted me, but now, I am not sure."

Varus places a hand on my shoulder. "When you win the games, surely she will see that you are the strongest and bravest of all males. She will see how worthy a mate you are; I am certain of it."

His words give me hope. "That is my desire, my prince."

Princess Lilliana strides into the room again. "Varus?"

His head snaps toward her. "Yes, my beloved?"

"I'm going to bed. Will you be coming soon?"

"I must go to bed." His eyes shine with happiness as he looks to Lilliana. "My mate needs me to keep her warm."

He moves past me and scoops her into his arms. She laughs as he tucks her close to his chest.

They seem so happy; I am glad for them both. My gaze dips to the swell of her abdomen, and my thoughts turn to Holly. Would that she was mine and carrying our fledgling. I would love nothing more than to start a family with her.

When I return to my chambers, I move to the balcony and peer at the sky.

My Holly came from the stars. I have never had a desire to visit space; the few times I have, I longed to return home. Yet I will take my place among them to prove to my female that I am worthy to be her mate. I would do anything to call her mine.

CHAPTER 16

HOLLY

W hen I return to my room, I collapse back onto the bed with a huff. I cannot believe that I just did that. I shouldn't have kissed Rakan. He doesn't want me.

Thank goodness he stopped me before we went any further. Before he did something he would regret, like bonding with me. His people mate for life, and I'm sure he would hate being bound to me for eternity.

I just… I thought he felt for me like I do for him. He's so thoughtful, kind, intelligent, and so handsome. I couldn't help but fall for him. He's everything I could ever want in a partner. However, I know that I am far from the ideal mate for him. He's a warrior, and I'm a teacher. I'm nothing like the women of his kind.

Since the Harvest Games were announced, all the unbonded Drakarian women have been talking about at school is how perfect a mate Rakan would be. Even though the men greatly outnumber the women in this world, it's obvious he can have whomever he chooses. So, why would he ever want me?

With a heavy sigh, I curl up beneath the covers and close my eyes, hoping I'll somehow be able to fall asleep. I have to get up early in the morning so I can slip away before he's awake. I know he wants to talk, but I already got the message loud and clear. I crossed a line. I kissed him and tried to push for more even though he doesn't want me.

I want to avoid the awkward *Can we just be friends?* conversation with him for as long as I can. I turn onto my stomach and bury my face in my pillow with a low groan. I am not looking forward to having *that* talk.

When I wake, the early morning rays of the sun are just barely peeking above the horizon. I quickly dress and make my way to the castle kitchens. I snag a mug of tea from the staff as well as a biscuit smothered with *kinril* and head into the city.

I reach the school and begin prepping the children's learning pods as Lurila has taught me. She walks over and assesses my work. "Excellent, Holly. You are picking this all up much faster than I anticipated."

Her praise is a bright start to my day until I catch a glimpse of her tablet. The screen is locked on an image of Rakan. He's been all over the vid feeds lately since he's favored to win the first leg of the Harvest Games held in Fire Clan territory.

She catches me eyeing her tablet and smiles. "He's a strong male, don't you agree?"

"Yes."

Clenching my jaw, I force myself not to roll my eyes. She's obviously into him, but I just wish she'd stop talking about it. I shouldn't be jealous. Lurila has been nothing but kind to me since we started working together. She's an excellent mentor and a good friend. Rakan deserves a mate like her.

I shouldn't be upset with her. It's not her fault that I'm not exactly the type a strapping warrior like Rakan would want as a mate.

"Soon, the harvest moon will be upon us," she continues. "It is thought to be a night blessed by the gods themselves. It is a good time to choose and claim a mate, Holly."

I think of Rakan and how she wants him to pursue her in the mating chase. As much as I wish she didn't want him and hope that he doesn't want her… she *is* a good person. So is he. I want only happiness for them both.

"I don't think I'll be choosing anyone, Lurila," I say sadly. "The only guy I want… he wants somebody else."

She blinks. "Are you certain?"

I look at her and sigh heavily. "Yes."

"Have you talked to him about this?"

I shake my head. "I can't. I already know he likes someone else… and I'll just end up making things awkward between us if I tell him how I feel."

She sits back in her chair. "You humans are very odd when it comes to choosing a mate."

"What do you mean?"

"For us… if we are interested in someone, we tell them outright. If they desire us in turn, then we begin the mating chase. At the end of it, the female decides if he is the one she wants or not."

"Like how you offered to meet Rakan?" I ask.

She nods. "It is best to approach such things directly, Holly. That way if you know a male is not interested, you can simply move on to someone else."

It seems so simple, the way she describes it. So, why does

it feel so impossible to do? There's no way I could just tell Rakan that I love him. I'm too afraid of rejection.

"Another oddity among your kind is the way females interact with one another. Most females feel threatened if another wants the male they desire, but you do not. You have never held it against me that I offered myself to Rakan, and I am glad, for I would not wish to lose your friendship over this."

Her statement stuns me. She knew I liked Rakan, but she still offered herself to him anyway. At first, I'm angry. But then, I realize this is just part of their culture. How could I hold it against her? The Drakarians are blunt and obvious about these things. She didn't do this to slight me. She simply did it because that's what they do when they want someone. They tell them outright.

"Well," I begin. "Some human women would be... aggressive, I suppose, but not me. You're my friend, and so is he. I only want what's best for you both. If that happened to be each other, then I would wish you well."

"Truly?" she asks.

"Truly," I reply.

She smiles. "Your species is not what we thought you were."

"What does that mean?"

"You may be fewer than our kind in number, but you have already changed this world in so many ways. All for the better." She pauses. "It has been many cycles since the Clans were peaceful, and after the recent peace summit and Harvest Games, we are united in a way we have not been since the ancient times of our people."

I never considered this, but she's right. Before we arrived, the Clans were all on the edge of war, except for the Earth Clan, of course. Apparently, they've always been neutral and never take sides in disputes.

"I am glad your people came to our world," she adds. "You have truly been a blessing from the gods."

A bright smile lights my face. "Thank you, Lurila."

The rest of the day passes by easily. As we check in on each fledgling's learning pod, it seems my programs are running smoothly. During midday meal, the children and my fellow teachers are all focused on the upcoming games and the festival. Everyone is looking forward to the festivities.

Everyone but me, that is. I'm dreading them because I already know that Rakan will win. He'll win, then he'll be gone. Forever.

My gaze drifts to Lurila, and my heart sinks even further. There's a chance Rakan might go to her during the harvest moon, chase her across the desert, and claim her as his mate.

Despite our earlier conversation, I can't help but wish so desperately that he doesn't go to her. But then again, why wouldn't he? She's beautiful, strong and... everything a Drakarian man would look for in a mate.

When I return to the castle, Lilliana greets me at the door. "I've been waiting for you."

"What for?"

She smiles. "I need your help with the decorations for the Harvest Festival and Games."

"All right," I agree.

She loops her arm through mine, and we make our way to the main hall to discuss our plans. When we reach it, I'm surprised to find all sorts of banners and decorations scattered across the tables.

"I'd like to hang these throughout the castle." She gestures to a table covered in long strings of festive lights.

When she asked me to help decorate, I didn't realize we

would begin right away. One of the guards, Tarok—Rakan's second in command—comes in. He bows before Lilly. "Prince Varus mentioned that you needed assistance," he says.

She smiles. "Yes, would you help us hang these lights?"

"Gladly." He grins. "I'm looking forward to the festival. The last time they were held, I was only a child, but I remember what great fun we had watching the games."

"You're going to participate in them, too," Lilly says.

He dips his chin. "Yes, Princess. I will be fighting against Rakan, though I doubt I will beat him."

My heart stutters at the mere mention of Rakan's name. We still haven't spoken since our kiss. "Why do you say that?"

"Because he is the strongest and fiercest of all warriors, my lady."

"You can call me Holly."

"Holly." He repeats my name solemnly. "It is a lovely name."

I smile. "Thank you."

Rakan walks in, and I don't miss the way he narrows his eyes at Tarok before he turns his attention back to me. "What are you doing?"

"Tarok offered to help me decorate the castle with Lilly so we can get everything ready for the harvest festival and games."

He turns to Tarok. "You are needed in the tower. *I* will help Holly to decorate."

A grin tugs at Tarok's mouth, and he nods to Rakan. Tarok turns back to me and flashes a handsome smile. "If you need anything else, please do not hesitate to ask me, Holly."

I return his smile. "Thank you, Tarok."

Rakan demands, "Why did you not ask me to help you?"

"You weren't around."

"I am always around," he says. "All you need do is ask for me, and someone will find me if I am not nearby."

"Well, someday you might not be," I counter.

He blinks. "Why do you say this?"

"If you win the tournament, you'll have to leave, won't you?"

"Yes, but I will return every six turns of the moon."

I purse my lips. "Great," I drawl. "So, I'll just wait until you come back every six months if I need something done."

He tilts his head to the side. "You are upset."

"No, I'm not," I lie because I know that I shouldn't be. I have no right to be upset. Whatever he chooses to do, it's not my place to judge or berate him.

"You *are* upset," he presses. "I can see it in your eyes. The thought of me winning displeases you somehow."

"Well, of course, it does." I sigh. "I don't want you to win, Rakan. If you win—"

"Tarok loses," he grumbles. "I see. You want him to be victorious because you desire him as your mate."

My head jerks back. "What?"

A muscle in his jaw ticks, his nostrils flare, and his gaze drops to the floor. "Tarok is a good male. You have… chosen well," he grinds out. "I understand now why you…"

"Why I what?" I prompt him when he trails off.

He grimaces. "It does not matter."

"Yes, it does," I insist. "Tell me."

He lowers his gaze. "I want to be…" He hesitates as if searching for the right words before continuing, "A good friend to you, Holly."

His words hit me like a physical blow. I should never have tried to touch him like I did last night. I crossed the line of friendship and I shouldn't have.

"You are, Rakan." I take his hand and meet his red eyes. "I want to be a good friend to you, too."

He smiles, but it does not touch his eyes. "You already are, Holly." He pauses. "Would you like to continue your lessons?" he asks, changing the subject.

I force myself to smile in return despite my sadness. "That would be great."

CHAPTER 17

RAKAN

Holly is brilliant. She has picked up our language so quickly, I am amazed at her intellect. Even her accent is perfect; she sounds just like one of our people. This is one of the many reasons why she will make an excellent teacher. She is tenacious and works diligently to master whatever challenge is presented to her.

She could live an easy life on Drakaria. We do not expect the humans to make a living here. When we took them in, we were prepared to provide for them indefinitely. It is no burden to take care of our newcomers, for we are a planet rich in wealth and resources. None of our Clans want for anything.

Yet, she still wants to contribute not only to our society but also to our future. As a teacher, she will mold the minds of future generations of Drakarians. It is a noble endeavor, and I admire her greatly for it.

We talked for many hours before she fell asleep on my

shoulder on a bench in the gardens. The air is growing colder now. When she shivers against me, I extend my wing and wrap it around her to share my warmth.

She lies against me so trustingly it nearly breaks me. After I failed her during the Wind Clan's attack, I feared she would never trust me again to keep her safe. A Drakarian female certainly would not. However, as my gaze travels over her form, I am acutely aware of the fact that she is not Drakarian.

Gently, I brush a stray tendril of her long, silken hair back from her face. Its color reminds me of the golden rays of sunlight that reflect in the river below during the day. Her skin is petal-soft, and as I eye her blunt nails, I cannot help but worry for her. Perhaps I feel so protective of her because she lacks natural defenses, though I doubt that is the only reason.

I glance down at my chest, half expecting the fated mark to appear. My instincts insist that she is mine. I have not told her this because I do not want to scare her or have her reject me outright.

Prince Kaj's mate, Anna, did not take the news very well at first, and Prince Llyr's mate, Talia, did not believe his assurance that they were fated until his fate mark finally appeared.

Holly is human just like their mates, and I do not want to alarm her by proclaiming something she may doubt or dislike. I must prove my worth to her first.

I know many of our males wait until the fated mark appears before choosing a mate. After all, it is the greatest honor we can receive from the gods—a sign that the bonding will always be blessed.

Even if my fate mark never appears for Holly... even if she was not my fated one, I would still desire her. I believe in making my own fate and my hearts and soul choose her.

I tighten my hold on Holly and am pleased when she

nestles further into my side. Everything within me insists she is mine. I yearn to tell her this even though I cannot.

Besides, her interaction with Tarok demonstrated that she is still searching for a potential mate.

Tarok is a good male, but I do not know if he would be right for her. He is charismatic, much like Prince Varus, but he is also prone to making jokes—more often than is sometimes appropriate. When he first began training, the habit got him into trouble, but he has learned to temper his humor since then.

Carefully, I lift her into my arms and carry her to her room. I do not wish to wake her, for I know she has been studying and working tirelessly lately.

When I reach her room, I quietly push open the door and gently tuck her beneath the covers. I'm pleased when she clings to me reluctantly as I pull away.

Her eyes blink open and she gives me a sleepy smile. "Did you carry me to bed?" she asks.

"You fell asleep, and I did not wish to wake you."

She yawns and turns on her side to face me as I tuck the comforter over her shoulder. She closes her eyes and snuggles into the covers. "I must be dreaming," she murmurs.

"You are not," I tell her.

"You always say that in my dreams." She closes her eyes. "Goodnight, Rakan."

I still. She dreams of me? Often, even, if I can believe her sleepy words.

Hope fills me anew. If I can win the tournament and prove myself... maybe then, she will want me.

On my way down the hallway to my chambers, I encounter Tarok. Unable to stop myself, I narrow my eyes.

He laughs. "Do not glare at me, Rakan. I know better than to try to take your female."

His answer stuns me. "How did you know that I desire her?"

He arches a brow. "It is obvious," he states. "To everyone but her, it would seem."

"You are wrong. She knows, but she does not want me."

"Are you certain about that?"

"I—"

"She spends time with you, Rakan. She even goes out of her way to do so."

"I am teaching her our language."

He scoffs. "I have heard her speak Drakarian well enough to pass for one of our people now. She does not need to continue her lessons with you."

I blink. He's right.

"Yet, she does so because she seems to enjoy your company. Above all others, I might add. Human females are known to seek out time with a male when they are interested in mating him."

I cross my arms over my chest and study him for a moment. "How is it that you know so much about human females?"

He tips his chin up with pride. "I ask them. I am preparing for my trip into space to help search for the rest of their people. I want to understand as much as I can about humans in case I find my fated one among them. I must be prepared to know how to properly woo her."

Underneath his light-hearted, teasing demeanor, he is astonishingly wise. Yet one thing he said bothers me. I arch a brow. "Do you really believe that you will best me in the games and win the chance to board the deep-space ships?"

"I am positive that I will best you." He grins. "But not because I am the better fighter."

My brow furrows. How does he expect to win if he cannot beat me in the games?

He claps a hand on my shoulder. "I will see you in the morning."

CHAPTER 18

HOLLY

I searched for Rakan this morning to invite him to tea, but I couldn't find him. The harvest moon is approaching, and I'm desperate to talk to him. I must tell him how I feel. I don't want him to go into the desert with Lurila or anyone else, for that matter, and perform the mating chase beneath the harvest moon.

If he's going to chase anyone, I want it to be me. I know it's crazy to think he might be interested in me like that, but I've decided that I have nothing to lose. I know him. He's an excellent warrior, and he's going to win the Harvest Games. When he does, I will lose him forever, *unless* I tell him how I feel beforehand.

When afternoon break arrives, I go outside to play with the children. Now that I've taught them how to play hide and seek, it's all they want to do.

I close my eyes and begin counting down while the fledglings hide on the playground.

Alarms begin blaring throughout the city, and my eyes

snap open. Panic tightens my chest. The last time the alarms rang, the Wind Clan attacked. I whip my head toward Lurila, who rushes out of the building. "What's going on?"

"A sandstorm is approaching the city. We must get everyone inside. Now!"

Several other teachers file out of the building and begin calling for the children to come in. Just as we think the last one's inside, one boy turns to me. "Miss Holly?"

"Yes?"

"Kovan is still outside."

"What?" I demand. "Where?"

"Over there." She points to a grouping of boulders at the far end of the playground. "He was too scared to come in."

"Stay inside," I tell her. "I'll go get Kovan."

A gust of wind whips around my body, pulling my hair free of its tie. The long blond strands swirl around me, impairing my vision but I brush them away. A fine haze of red surrounds me as the grit and crimson sand of the desert scratches at my skin. I peer into the distance, and my heart drops when I see a solid, dark wall rushing toward the city.

The air is thick with dust, and I fist my sleeve, placing it over my mouth and nose to help me breathe as I creep toward the boulders.

"Kovan!" I scream into the wind, but he doesn't answer.

My heart hammers in my chest. Varus has stressed many times how dangerous the sandstorms are. Prince Raidyn—Skye's husband—was caught in one as a child. The storm killed his mother and would have killed him as well if not for the Healers who found them and saved his life.

Terror fills me as the wind picks up and fine sand rips at my skin like blades, but I can't turn back. I cannot leave a child stranded in this terrible storm.

When I finally reach the boulders, I find Kovan hiding in

between the rocks in a small space barely big enough for two people.

"Kovan!" I shout, and his little head snaps up, his eyes swimming with tears. "Are you all right?"

"I'm scared, Miss Holly," he whimpers.

I kneel and wrap my arms around his trembling form. "It's all right. I'm here, Kovan."

The rock surrounding us blocks enough of the wind that I can lift my head and turn my gaze back toward the school. The air is so thick with sand, I cannot see any further than my outstretched hand at this point. We can't go back; we'll never make it through the onslaught.

I turn back to Kovan and his tiny shelter between the rocks. "Can you crawl any further in?" I ask.

He shakes his head.

Grains of sand scrape my skin like sharp needles. I push as close to Kovan as I can, but my back is still relatively exposed. My robe protects me from the worst of the storm, though, and I'm at least grateful that I can use my body to shield Kovan's.

I would sooner die than allow him to come to any harm.

He snuggles into my embrace, his tiny form trembling with fear against mine. The wind picks up, and the air grows so clogged with sand that all light of the sun is blocked and the world is nearly pitch black. Tears sting my eyes, and I grit my teeth as the sand grates across my back. The pain is blindingly intense, but I refuse to move. I must shield Kovan.

The wind howls all around us, drowning out his panicked wails. I try to soothe him, but I'm in agony. I'm certain my robe has been torn off my back because my skin feels like it's on fire.

Closing my eyes, I focus on breathing in and out as I grip him tightly.

"Miss Holly," he whimpers. "I smell blood. Are you hurt?"

"Shhh," I tell him. "It's all right. I'll keep you safe, Kovan."

He sobs into my robe. "I don't want you to get hurt, Miss Holly."

"Shhh," I try to soothe him again. "It's all right, Kovan."

I think of Rakan and pray that he is safe. I think of my family and all of my friends, hoping they are as well. Tears stream down my face as agonizing pain sears across my skin. The wind howls all around us, clawing at my form and trying to pull me from the rocks.

It's so loud I can no longer hear Kovan's small cries even as he continues to shake in my arms. I grit my teeth, struggling to remain conscious even as the darkness beckons me into the welcoming void of oblivion, away from all of this fear and pain.

Warmth blooms across my back and I wonder how much damage has been done to my body, for I recognize that this is blood. I shudder inwardly as terrible images steal through my mind of my injuries.

The wind howls, ripping at my form. No matter how much I want only to allow myself to pass out to escape this pain, I cannot. If I did, it would sure pull me away. Completely out in the open, I'd have no chance at all of survival.

I close my eyes and picture King Raidyn—Skye's husband and mate, and the terrible scare on his face. He got it when he was caught out in a sandstorm and now that I understand what they are, I realize how strong he must have been to survive this.

My heart clenches as I think of Rakan. He believes that I'm brave and strong. I have to hold on, I cannot let go. His words repeat in my mind: *"You are brave and you are strong, Holly."*

A broken sob escapes me as I imagine his face. I wish he were here right now. I should have told him how I felt. I love him and now, he'll never know. I'll die without giving him the truth deep in my soul. I love him more than anyone or anything in this world. And I'm a coward for never telling him.

The storm seems to go on forever as pain burns like fire across my back. Kovan trembles in my arms, holding tightly to me. I cannot let go and I can't fail him. I have to keep him safe.

The wind slowly begins to die down. My entire body trembles and aches. My muscles burn in protest from holding onto the rocks and to Kovan. My back feels as if it's been seared. I'm in so much pain, I can barely think straight.

A panicked voice rises behind me. "Holly! Kovan!"

Warm hands alight on my shoulders and carefully pull me away from the rock. I blink up to find Rakan leaning over me. "Holly!"

I reach my trembling arm up to cup his face. "Rakan," I barely manage. "You found me."

"Holly." He brushes the hair back from my face, his red eyes full of panic. He gathers me close his chest. "Oh, Holly. Hang on, I'm going to take you to the Med Center. Healer Ranas will be able to heal you."

I brush my thumb across his lower lip and speak the words that I was too afraid to ever utter before. "I love you," I whisper. "I want you to know in case I—"

Unable to stand the pain any longer, I close my eyes, and my head falls back as I spiral into oblivion.

CHAPTER 19

RAKAN

Alarms blare throughout the city as my fellow Fire Clan warriors and I usher as many civilians into the palace and surrounding buildings as we can. We seal the windows and doors as the solid dark wall of the sandstorm looms in the distance, rapidly approaching.

My thoughts turn to Holly. She's at school, but I wish desperately that she were here. Rationally, I know she will be safe sheltering in that building. Like all structures built within Fire Clan territory, the schoolhouse can withstand these storms. Even so, I wish she were close by, where I could see her and make certain that she is safe.

As soon as every opening is closed and the palace is locked down, I go to Prince Varus. I want his permission to leave and find Holly as soon as this is over. Surely he'll understand.

"Prince Varus," I call when I find him in the throne room with his mate.

"Yes?"

I bow low. "The premises are sealed. I have no doubt we will weather the storm just fine."

"Excellent," he replies. "Thank you, Rakan."

I straighten. "I would ask your permission to leave for the school once the winds die down so I may check on Holly."

"Of course."

Princess Lilliana's eyes widen. "Is it safe at the school?"

I nod as he turns to her. "Yes, my beloved. She should be safe. All our buildings are built to withstand these storms."

Even though his words make sense, I cannot quiet the unrest in my heart. I feel as if something is wrong. Absently, I rub my hand across my chest as a deep ache settles directly over my hearts, where my fate mark should be glowing for her.

I wait near the entrance to the castle as the storm ravages the city. The air is so thick with sand and grit, I cannot see farther than an arm's length through the shielded glass. My hearts pound in my chest as I wait for it to pass.

Closing my eyes, I picture Holly's beautiful face, her lovely blue eyes, and her long golden hair spilling down her back and over her shoulders. She has never weathered a sandstorm before. They can often last for days, but this is one of the rare ones that approaches without much warning and moves through quickly. The storm should be gone momentarily, but it will not be soon enough for me.

Tarok sprints toward me. "Rakan!"

"What is it?" I turn to face him, dread paralyzing me when I notice the panic that mars his expression. "Teacher Lurila from the school is on the vidscreen for you. She says it is urgent."

I rush toward the communication room, desperate to reach it quickly. She's lucky she was able to get a signal through to us while the storm is still moving through. I do not know how long it will hold. I don't want the call to cut off before I reach her.

When I enter the room, Prince Varus and Princess Lilliana are already there. Varus is holding Lilliana close as she sobs into his chest.

"What is it?" I demand, not bothering to hide my alarm. "What has happened?"

Lurila speaks through the vidscreen, tears in her eyes. "Holly went outside as the storm hit. She went to retrieve one of the missing fledglings."

"Is she all right?"

"We do not know. They did not make it back. They're both caught out in the storm. And I fear they may be—" her breath hitches as tears fall down her cheeks. "There is no way they could possibly survive this," she sobs. "It's all my fault."

My hearts stop in my chest as ice shoots through my veins.

I turn to Varus, and he nods, already knowing what I seek.

I throw a large, hooded cape over my back. The material is thick and should provide some protection against the storm. I pull the face shield on top to protect my eyes and make my way to the door.

Tarok pulls at my arm, alarm raising his voice. "What are you doing?"

"I'm going to find Holly."

"You cannot go out in this storm, Rakan!" he calls out.

I ignore his warning. I have no time to waste, so I push my way through the doors and head out into the storm. I will save Holly, or I will die trying.

The wind howls and tears at my form as I stalk down the cobbled pathway toward the school. I dare not fly since I know it could easily throw me around and damage my wings. I have no way to protect them from the sand.

I have seen what happens to those caught in sandstorms without protection. Their scales are scraped raw by the sharp grains of sand, exposing the tissue beneath. It is pain I would not wish on even my worst enemy.

I shudder inwardly. Holly's skin is fragile compared to a Drakarian's scales. I fear for the fledgling, as well; their scales are not as developed nor as hard as an adult's. I pray they are both somehow safe and sheltered. I cannot bear to think otherwise.

My pulse pounds in my ears as I make my way through the storm. When I reach the edge of the school, I head straight for the play area. The same place that, not long ago, Holly and I shared a picnic midday meal. Clenching my jaw, I force myself to focus beyond my horror and trepidation. I must find her and the fledgling. That is my only task for now.

A flash of movement catches the corner of my eye. Bridon emerges from the school, wearing a cape similar to mine.

"They were last seen going toward those rocks," he shouts above the din, pointing into the distance to a group of boulders.

Together, we make the difficult trek there. As we approach, my nostrils flare when I detect the scent of blood on the wind. Not just any blood—human blood. I recognize the scent easily from the day so many of them were injured during the Wind Clan's attack on the city.

My hearts pound as I follow the scent. When I reach the boulders, I inhale sharply.

Her body is shivering, and her back is completely exposed. The wind has torn her robe from her body, the shreds clinging to her form. Instead of its normal pale coloring, her skin is raw and red with blood—almost as red as the scales of my Fire Clan brethren.

I rush toward her, calling her name but receiving no response. She is wrapped around a fledgling who lifts his head to peer up at me with wide eyes. "Miss Holly saved me. She passed out. You must help her. She's hurt."

Bridon grabs the fledgling as I gather Holly into my arms. "Holly!"

Her eyes open and she reaches a trembling hand up to cup his face. "Rakan," she barely manages. "You found me."

My hearts clench. "Holly." I brush the hair back from her face and hold her close to my chest. "Oh, Holly. Hang on, I'm going to take you to the Med Center. Healer Ranas will be able to heal you."

She brushes her thumb across my lower lip as her blue eyes stare deep into mine. "I love you," she whispers. "I want you to know in case I—"

Her head falls back and she falls unconscious. I wrap my cape solidly around us both as I rush to the Med Center.

She slumps in my arms with a stillness that unnerves me, but I force myself to press on. I cannot stop, for I know the only way to help her is to find Healer Ranas. As a member of the Earth Clan, his healing fire should be able to heal her.

Eternity seems to pass before we reach the doors. They are sealed shut due to the storm, so I pound my fist against the protective glass.

Healer Ranas answers immediately, ushering me inside. Grains of sand follow me in, scraping across the floor before he seals the doors shut behind us.

His golden eyes search mine frantically. "What has happened?"

I throw off my cape, revealing Holly's injured form. I lay her on the table, and he gasps when he catches sight of her back. Her skin is torn and shredded from her body, revealing the raw, bleeding tissue beneath.

She doesn't move or make a sound, and her stillness terrifies me. "Holly?"

Ranas runs the scanner over her body, studying the readings. He proceeds to blow blue-green healing fire across her back.

Her eyes snap open, and she wails in pain as he shifts her slightly to reach another area.

I touch her cheek. "Holly, you are safe."

Tears drip down her cheeks as she rolls to her side, facing me. "It burns." Her voice shakes with sobs. "It's so painful."

Her anguish tears at my hearts as she hold my hand tightly. My nostrils flare. The blooming scent of her blood sparks fear deep inside me.

I grip her hand to ground her and speak in soothing tones. "You will be well, Holly. Healer Ranas is mending you."

"Rakan," she gasps. "Is Kovan safe?"

My hearts clench. She is strong. Despite her pain, she worries about the fledgling she sheltered and saved. "Yes. He is fine, thanks to you."

"Thank goodness," she whimpers. "I was so worried."

I gently brush the hair from her face. "You will be well. The pain should subside soon."

More tears roll down her cheeks. The healing flame of the Earth Clan causes drowsiness in humans. As Ranas completes his work, her eyelids flutter, and she struggles to stay awake.

"Are you feeling any better?" I ask.

She nods and gently squeezes my hand. "Will you stay with me?" she whispers.

I hold her deep-blue gaze. "Always."

CHAPTER 20

HOLLY

As my mind slowly resurfaces to awareness, I'm surrounded by warmth. I shift slightly, surprised to find my back no longer hurts. The last thing I remember is intense pain before I fell unconscious—and Rakan's red eyes searching mine as I struggled to stay awake.

Something tightens around my waist. My eyes snap open, and I look down to find that I'm wrapped up in red-orange wings. A faint smile curves my mouth when I realize it must be Rakan.

Carefully, I turn in his arms to face him. His red eyes are already open.

"You are awake." He breathes out a sigh of relief. Tenderly, he rests his forehead against mine and closes his eyes. "I prayed to the gods over and over that you would awaken soon. You slept so long I was worried."

"What happened?" I ask.

"I found you using your body to shield the fledgling from

the sandstorm. I brought you to the Med Center, and Ranas blew his healing fire over your back."

I shift slightly in his arms. His expression remains grave, and worry blooms in my chest. "What is it?"

"The damage to your skin was severe, Holly. The tissue has knit together, but it is heavily scarred."

I lower my eyes as I process this grim news. A tear slips down my cheek as I think on my ruined flesh. King Raidyn—Skye's mate—has a scar on his face and Skye said he was always looked down upon by females because they did not want a disfigured mate.

Now, I have scars all across my back. Rakan will never want me.

Rakan cups my face, tracing the soft pad of his thumb across my skin. "Does it still hurt, Holly?"

I choke back a sob. "No. How ugly is it?"

His red eyes meet mine evenly. "You are not ugly, Holly. You are the most beautiful female I have ever seen. The bravest, smartest, kindest—"

"It's all right, Rakan," I murmur. "You don't need to make me feel better, though I appreciate the attempt. You're a good friend."

CHAPTER 21

RAKAN

"Y ou're a good friend," she says, and her words tear at my hearts. I want to be more than a friend to her. I want to be her mate.

She closes her eyes as more tears begin to fall.

I pull her close. "Please, do not cry, Holly. I am speaking the truth. I would not lie to you."

I stroke her cheek. "You are brave and selfless. You saved Kovan, Holly. He might have died if not for your strength and your sacrifice."

"I'm not strong, Rakan."

"Yes, you are." I cup her chin and tip her face up to mine. "You are one of the bravest people I have ever known."

She hugs me. "You saved me. Again."

Her words rekindle guilt in my chest. I am the reason she was hurt before, during the attack by the Wind Clan. Yet... she does not hold that against me, and I will not point out that I failed her then. I am more resolved than ever to win the Harvest Games and show her that I am worthy to be hers.

She nestles further into me. "You're so warm."

I brush the hair back from her face. "I tried to lay you down in your bed, but you would not let me go. I did not mean to impose upon you."

She smiles. "It's no imposition. I like spending time with you."

Happiness blooms in my chest. Perhaps all is not lost. She likes me, and she trusts me to take care of and hold her. Once I win the games and prove that I am a worthy male, I will ask her to be my mate. I only pray that she agrees.

"The games begin in two days," I declare proudly.

She stills. "That's when the harvest moon rises too, right?"

"Yes."

"Are you going to—" She breaks off, licking her lips nervously. "You're still going to participate in the games?"

"Of course. It is a great honor to compete, and an even greater one to win."

She lifts her gaze to me. "You really want to go into space?"

I nod, even though it is not the truth; I merely wish to impress her. I actually dislike space. The few times I've gone, I longed to return home. However, it is not as if I will remain there forever once I win. Each Drakarian chosen for this duty must serve only three cycles before they can choose to return home permanently. Even during service, they may come home on leave every six turns of the moon. "I will visit you when I am on leave, Holly."

Her faint smile does not touch her eyes, and I worry that she may not want me to visit. After all, she may have her eye on another male as her choice of mate. My thoughts drift to Tarok. I can hardly bear the thought of her with another— even someone as honorable as him.

Although I wish to stay here and hold her all day long, I have duties I must attend. I must guard Prince Varus so that Tarok can have some time off. After all, he's been covering for me ever since I found Holly injured. I'm sure he must be tired.

I brush another stray lock of hair back from her face, studying her lovely features and committing them to memory. I want to remember this moment long after I am gone, searching deep space for her kin. I will think of her and miss her every single day once I leave.

CHAPTER 22

HOLLY

"I must go attend to my duties," he says. "Do you need anything before I leave?"

I shake my head. "Thank you for caring for me. I remember asking you to stay with me when I was in the Med Center. Thank you for everything, Rakan."

He smiles. "All you need do is ask, and I will always stay with you, Holly."

I open my mouth to speak, wanting to ask him to stay with me forever. To forget about the games and start a life here on Drakaria with me. However, as I meet his red eyes, the words die in my throat. He's so excited about winning these games. I can't take that away from him when it means so much.

If I asked, he'd probably stay just for me, but then... how long before he begins to resent me for making him sacrifice his dreams? I can't do it. No matter how much I love him and want him by my side, I won't do that to him.

An old Earth saying comes to mind: *If you love someone, let them go.* If the one I love comes back to me, he is mine and always was. If he doesn't, then it's not meant to be.

Watching Rakan leave the room, I finally understand what I must do. I love him. So, I must let him go. Whether he chooses Lurila or a trek into space… the choice must be his. I cannot decide for him nor ask him to sacrifice for me.

A sudden knock at my door startles me. I stand from the bed and wrap my robe around my form. "Enter," I call out.

The door opens to reveal a smiling Lurila. "You're up and about. This is excellent."

Her nostrils flare, and her gaze drops to the bed. Her eyes flick back up to me, a question behind them. "Rakan was here?"

I nod. "He took care of me after I was injured."

Sadness fills me as my mind returns unbidden to the mating chase invitation she extended to Rakan.

Quickly, I change the subject. "How is Kovan?"

The smile returns to her face. "Alive because of your bravery, Holly. His parents wanted me to give this to you."

She hands me a small parcel.

"What is this?"

I open it to find a dagger inside. The handle is beautifully carved and encrusted with gemstones. It's lovely, though this is clearly a dangerous weapon. The sharpened blade glints beneath the overhead lighting. I search Lurila's face, frowning.

"His mother is a weapons crafter. She made this dagger especially for you. It is… an honor to be gifted such a fine weapon. They are immeasurably grateful that you saved their son and have asked me to convey that they are forever indebted to you."

I smile. "They owe me nothing. Tell them I appreciate the gift, however."

I place the parcel on a side table. How strange to give such a deadly gift, but then, the Drakarians are a race of warriors.

"I'm uncertain if you are aware, but school has been suspended until after the Harvest Games."

I blink. These games are a much bigger deal than I realized if classes have been canceled. Drakarians take education very seriously. "The games are that important?"

She nods. "They have not been held in many cycles, so no one wants to miss this important event now. I'm certain most of Drakaria will be in attendance." She sighs and adds, "And I am certain Rakan will win. Everyone is. Victory will bring him even greater honor than he already has."

Her words make my heart clench and further my resolve not to say anything to Rakan. I cannot ask him to give up this opportunity for me when it means so much to him and Drakarian culture. I'll just have to pray that he loses, even though I know how unlikely my wish is.

He's the best warrior—of that, I am certain—but maybe I'll get lucky. Maybe he'll have an off day and accidentally lose.

I accompany Lurila to the gardens, where we find Lilly, Prince Varus, and of course, Rakan. As I introduce Lurila to Lilly and Varus, she turns to Rakan, and I don't miss the way her eyes travel appreciatively over his form.

He growls at her, and my heart sinks because the sound resembles the one Varus makes when he's kissing Lilly.

A deep aches settles in my chest. Tears sting my eyes, but I blink them back. I'm not going to cry. I am stronger than that. Rakan is my friend and so is Lurila. If they want each other, then I should be happy for them.

After all, it's not as if he's mine. When he found me, after the storm, I thought I'd told him that I love him, but it must have been a dream because he has said nothing about it since then.

What good would it do to tell him now? He wants Lurila, and now I suspect he's going to meet her in the desert. What am I going to do?

CHAPTER 23

HOLLY

The day of the festival finally arrives. A bright smile is plastered on Rakan's face as we drink tea during breakfast in the gardens.

"I will fight, and I will win this day. You will see," he declares.

My heart clenches. He wants to win so badly.

He cocks his head to the side. "If an honorable male wanted a human female to be his mate, is there anything else he should do besides declare it? Lilly was speaking to Varus about rings. She said it was a human tradition. Is this truth?"

I blink at him. I thought he wanted Lurila, but it seems he might still be hung up on one of my crew members.

I swallow against the lump in my throat and do my best to smile. "Yes. Humans often exchange rings when they bond. It's an old tradition, but some still do it."

He frowns and looks down at his hand. "I do not think a ring would work for a Drakarian male. It would not survive the shift to draka form."

I shrug. "Well, rings aren't for everyone, you know."

"What about you?" he asks. "Would you want a male to give you such a thing?"

"No. I would just want him to promise me forever." A wistful smile crests my lips. "That's all I would ever need."

"Easily done for a Drakarian male," he replies. "Our people mate for life."

I open my mouth to speak, but Lilly's voice rings out from across the garden.

"Holly? Do you want to accompany me to the festival?"

"Sure."

I glance back at Rakan. He flashes a handsome smile. "I must be off as well, to the arena. I will search for you in the stands."

I muster my cheeriest smile. "I'll be there."

He practically skips off, he's so excited. Prince Varus claps a hand on his shoulder before they both leave.

Lilly walks up to me. "Let's wander through the markets first and see what the vendors are selling. What do you say?"

Despite the horrible ache in my chest as I think of Rakan, I grin. "It sounds fun."

As we make our way down the main road, we pass stands laden with wares and food for the festival. The aroma of delicious meats and spices suffuses the air, enticing customers to buy various snacks and dishes.

I glance to the right and notice a stand selling handheld cakes slathered with *kinril*. Lilly gives me a knowing glance, and we head straight for it.

The Drakarian man running the stand smiles warmly at us in greeting. "You are my tenth human customers this day already," he says proudly.

I notice that one side of his stand holds cakes with *kinril* while the other side has cakes without. He's thoughtful to cater to us humans when there are so few of us. After all, only twenty-five of us made it onto this planet so far since none of the other escape pods have been found.

"Thank you for remembering us," Lilly says, having noticed the layout of his stand as well.

He bows. "You are most welcome, Princess Lilliana."

Warm hands on my shoulder draw my attention behind me, and I beam as soon as I see Rakan smiling.

"The contests will begin shortly. Be sure to get there with plenty of time to find a seat." He grins. "You will not want to miss me beating my opponents."

Prince Varus joins us and gathers Lilly into his arms. He places his palm over her abdomen, as he always seems to do lately. "I will fight and bring honor to you and our child, my mate."

She kisses him and smiles. "Be careful. I don't want you to get hurt."

He puffs out his chest and tips up his head. "I will not be hurt, my Lilly."

I take Rakan's hand. "You be careful too, all right?"

He frowns. "Do you doubt me?"

It's obvious that my question has somehow offended his pride, so I quickly reassure him, "No. I know you're going to win. I just... don't like that the fighting means someone could get hurt."

He cocks his head to the side. "I spar most days with my warriors."

He has a point, so I relent. "All right. Just—"

"I will watch for you from the stands." He flashes his grin again.

When he and Varus leave, Lilly takes my hand, bouncing with excitement. "You and Rakan are together now?"

I shrug. "No. It's... complicated."

"How so?"

"I mean… we're friends, and he took care of me after I was hurt in the sandstorm, but I'm confused. I used to be sure he wanted to pursue me, but after the Wind Clan attacked, everything changed. We became more like good friends, you know?"

She arches a brow. "It seems like you're more than just good friends to me."

I frown. "How so?"

"He is so excited for you to watch him in the games. Can't you see he's just like Varus? He's excited to prove himself to you, Holly. Aside from that, he's always spending time with you. Almost every free moment he has, in fact," she adds. "I don't think he'd do that for just a *friend*."

"Then why did he pull away after the Wind Clan attack? I don't get it."

She steps closer. "Have you two discussed your relationship?"

"No. I've been too afraid. A few days ago, we kissed, but he stopped me before we went any further. So, I figure he might have changed his mind. Or maybe I had it all wrong, to begin with."

"I don't think that's it. You should talk to him. Maybe something else is going on. You'd be surprised how differently Drakarians think, Holly. Their culture is so complex that quite a few misunderstandings still happen between me and Varus. That's why we must talk things through—to make sure we understand one another." She shakes her head. "I think you should do the same with Rakan. It can't hurt."

"Yes, but—" Tears spring to my eyes, but I blink them back.

"What's wrong?"

"If he wins, he'll be gone, and it won't matter anyway."

Her brow furrows with earnest concern. "I didn't

consider that. You need to talk to him, Holly. Do it before it's too late. Today is only the first round of the games. Talk to him after."

I nod reluctantly. "Even if he likes me… he's so excited to compete. Everyone knows he'll win. I don't want him to give up his dream for me, and then resent me later."

She sighs. "I'm sorry, Holly."

I lift my gaze to hers. "Is it wrong if I say that, deep down, I'm hoping he'll lose even though he wants to win so badly?"

"No, it isn't wrong if your motivation is that you want him to stay here with you." She smiles warmly, squeezing my hand. "Come on. Let's go to the stands. We can watch the games, and we'll both secretly be rooting for him to lose."

"All right."

When we reach the arena, I'm surprised by how closely it resembles old Earth images I've seen of the Coliseum in Rome. We make our way to the designated seating for Fire Clan royalty. Varus's parents are already there, and they greet me warmly. He's so blessed to still have both of his parents.

As people file in, we wave when we catch sight of Skye and her husband, King Raidyn, among the crowd. Prince Llyr and Talia accompany them, and Prince Kaj and Anna follow. Though we last saw them only weeks ago, all the years of living in close quarters on the ship have made those weeks apart feel like an eternity.

King Raidyn is so much larger than the others, and yet he's so gentle with Skye as he guides her to her seat. She places a hand over her slightly swollen abdomen, and a wistful sigh escapes me, imagining how happy they must be.

Talia is starting to show as well, and so is Anna. According to Lilly and Healer Ranas, they'll all have a short-ened pregnancy of six months instead of nine. Judging by how far along they all appear to be, I think he's right.

Talia places her hand lovingly over her baby bump as she

smiles at us. "We're certain we're having twins. Isn't that wonderful?"

Prince Llyr wraps his arm and wing around her side and presses a tender kiss to her temple. "We will have a son *and* a daughter."

I know Prince Llyr has a twin sister, Noralla. So, twins must run in his family. I hug Talia with sincere warmth. "I'm so happy for you."

"Thank you, Holly." Her gaze drifts down to the arena and the Drakarians lined up to participate in the games, including Rakan. "What about you? How are things between you and Rakan?"

"Are you officially courting yet?" Anna asks.

I sigh. "No. I'm... not sure he even wants me."

Prince Kaj frowns. "Of course, he does."

My eyes snap to him. "Why do you say that?"

"You are obviously the female he desires. What makes you doubt this?"

I lower my gaze. "One of the teachers I work with... offered to meet him in the desert for the mating chase. He..." I swallow against the lump in my throat. "Growled at her."

When he says nothing, I lift my gaze and find him staring at me with a deeply furrowed brow. "Was it a growl of acceptance, or one of refusal?"

My head jerks back. "There's a difference?"

He arches a brow. "Different growls mean different things."

I blink. I never knew that; to me, a growl is a growl. Hope flares inside me. I open my mouth to ask another question, but Varus's voice echoing over the speakers interrupts me. He announces the beginning of the games.

As I watch Rakan prepare to face down his first opponent, I resolve that I will ask him as soon as we leave today.

I must know how he feels about Lurila. I am desperate to know whether he rejected her or not.

CHAPTER 24

RAKAN

I defeat my first two opponents with ease. My second is Bridon, the teacher who works with Holly. I cannot deny the satisfaction I feel when I pin him to the ground within the first few minutes of the fight. If there was ever any doubt in his mind about who is the better male for Holly, I quickly erased it when I beat him.

He could never protect her as well as I could. When I offer him my hand to help him stand, he accepts with a grim nod. In his eyes, I read resignation, as well. I should feel sorry for him, but I cannot.

I can barely contain a satisfied grin as I glance up at the stands to find Holly watching in rapt attention. I'm glad she witnessed that I am the superior male. Hopefully, my actions here suffice to convince her of my ability to protect her and any fledglings we might have if she chooses me.

Tarok—my second-in-command—is my next opponent, and he will not be so easily beaten. I have trained him myself, so I know what a strong and capable warrior he is.

As we circle one another, his determined eyes meet mine. He is eager to prove himself, as well.

He lunges forward, and I duck to one side, swiping out with my tail. I knock his feet out from under him.

He slams to the ground but quickly recovers and jumps up to face me again. He feigns a left hit before kicking out. He hits my torso, but there isn't enough force behind the kick to knock me back. I rush toward him, then we are rolling on the ground in a tangled mess of limbs, claws, and fangs.

He is strong, but I am stronger. After what feels like forever, I pin him to the ground. Blood drips down my forehead from a tear in my scalp down my face, and I brush the sticky liquid from my eyes.

When the announcer calls the fight in my favor, I extend a hand and help him off the ground. He dips his chin in a show of respect.

"Well fought." He grins. "Tomorrow, I will fight better."

A teasing smirk twists my lips, and I narrow my eyes. Tomorrow, we will fight in draka form. I have no doubt I will beat him again. "We shall see."

He laughs and claps a hand on my shoulder as we walk back into the training area.

Night has fallen by the time I finish washing up. Healer Ranas enters to blow his healing flame over our injuries. We ask him to simply patch us up since we know he has many to treat this day and needs to conserve his energy.

My body hums with anticipation. I am eager to see Holly. She witnessed my triumph this day, and I can hardly wait to see her face light with joy when I approach.

As I leave the arena and push through the crowd, many nod in respect. I make my way to the great bonfire and watch with an absent smile as people dance around the flames and jubilantly celebrate the Harvest Games. So many cycles have come and gone since our last Harvest Games, but I remember these festivities well. I'm grateful for their return and hope they are here to stay.

I glance across the dancing crowd and find Holly seated beside Princess Lilliana and Prince Varus. King Raidyn, Prince Llyr, and Prince Kaj are all here, as well, with their human mates. I glance down at their mates' rounding abdomens with envy. I wish Holly were already mine and carrying our fledgling. I long to start a family with her.

Her head turns toward me, and I grin like the lovesick fool that I am. My expression falls at her disapproving frown, and I stride toward her.

Prince Varus stands and claps a hand on my shoulder. "Well fought this day, Rakan."

"Yes," Prince Kaj adds. "Your skills are impressive."

I drop into a sweeping bow. "Thank you, my Lords."

I turn my attention back to Holly. She wears a strange expression that I cannot quite discern.

I tilt my head to the side. "Is everything all right?"

She lowers her gaze. "Yes."

Despite her assurance, I know something is wrong. "May I speak to you?" I ask. "Privately."

She lifts her blue eyes to glance over my shoulder.

"Rakan?"

I spin to find Lurila—her coworker and friend—behind me. "Hello," I greet her.

"I wanted to congratulate you," she says. "The fledglings have talked of nothing but this event for days. They were excited that they got to meet you the other day. I was wondering if perhaps you might stop by the school again to speak with them?"

"Of course," I agree. Especially since it means I'll get to see Holly as well.

Speaking of...

I turn back to find she has disappeared. My gaze sweeps over the area and catches her walking in the distance toward the many courtesy tents set up for visitors to rest.

"Forgive me," I tell Lurila.

I do not bother to wait for her reply before I start racing toward Holly. "Holly, wait! Where are you going?"

"Away from here," she mutters, not bothering to turn around.

"I wish to speak with you."

She spins to face me, her thunderous expression perplexing me. "Don't you have somewhere to be?"

I blink at her in astonishment. "What are you—"

"Lurila is waiting, isn't she?"

"*Lurila?*"

She turns away, her shoulders shaking with emotion. Cautiously, I touch her arm. A broken sob escapes her, tearing at my hearts.

"Holly, what is wrong? Please tell me. I will do whatever I can to make it better."

"I have tried to be strong, but I—" Her voice hitches. "I can't do it. Please, Rakan." She turns to me, her luminous blue eyes brimming with tears. "Don't go."

"Go where?" I blurt. "What are you talking about?"

"Don't go to the edge of the desert to meet Lurila tonight. I'm begging you not to. I—I thought I was strong enough to just stand by"—another sob interrupts her words—"but I can't. I can't bear it. I don't want you to mate with her."

My hearts stutter and stop. She is jealous of another female... because she wants me for herself.

Happiness blooms in my chest.

I grip her chin, tilting her head up to mine. Her face is swollen and red, and her eyelids are puffy from her tears.

"Do you forgive me for failing you?"

"Failing me?" Her brow furrows softly. "What are you talking about?"

I look down at my hands. "It was my fault you were injured during the Wind draka attack. I know I am not worthy of you. That is why I have not declared my desire for you to become my mate. I must know... do you forgive me, Holly?"

She blinks several times. "That's why you pulled away from me?"

I nod.

"You didn't fail me, Rakan." She steps forward and cups my cheek, her blue eyes searching mine intently. "You saved me. How could you ever think otherwise?"

"You want me?" Hope flares inside me. "Truly?"

A stunning smile curves her lips. "More than anything."

Cautiously, I lean forward and brush my lips against hers.

She wraps her arms around me, and I lift her into my arms. Her legs encircle my waist, and I pull away to study her. "You are certain?"

She nods, and I capture her mouth with mine. She gasps when I roll my hips against hers, and I enter her mouth, curling my tongue around hers as I deepen our kiss.

A low moan escapes her as my stav lengthens and extends from my mating pouch. With her robe partially open, only the lacy fabric of her undergarments separates my stav from her entrance.

Wet heat seeps through the silk, and my nostrils flare as I scent her arousal. My need for her is maddening, but I do not want anyone to see us. It would be improper to mate with her out in the open, where there are so many onlookers.

Panting heavily, I pull back and drop my forehead to hers. She is panting too, and when her eyes meet mine, they are dark with desire.

"Hold tight to me," I whisper.

She nods, and I spread my wings and take flight. I race back to the castle. As soon as I land on my balcony, she presses her lips to mine in a fervent kiss that steals the breath from my lungs. I can barely walk in a straight line—or think, for that matter—but I somehow manage to stumble to the bed.

We fall onto the comforter in a tangled mess of limbs as I crush my lips to hers. She moans into my mouth as I slide my hand down her torso, carefully loosening the fabric of her robe. I am desperate to feel her bare skin against mine. I want to gaze upon her beauty, and I want nothing separating us.

This is everything I have desired. I long to claim her as mine and be claimed in return.

"I want to see you," I rasp.

Her hands find mine, and she helps me undo the fastening of her robe, pulling it free from her body and leaving her naked beneath me.

I survey her in wonder. As my gaze travels over the silken scrap of fabric around her breasts and between her thighs, I note they are the same items I brought her days ago from the tailor. I remember her telling me that a female will remove her clothing when she is willing to mate.

She pulls the fabric free, revealing the soft, creamy mounds of her breasts. My mouth waters with the urge to take them into my mouth. I long to run my tongue over her entire body. She takes my hand and rests my open palm over her breast.

Her body is so soft and giving. I brush my thumb over the peak, and I'm surprised to feel it harden to a bead. Her cheeks flare a lovely shade of red as her blue eyes stare up into mine.

"I chose this color,"—she gestures to the silken fabric

—"because they match your scales." Shyly, she bites her lower lip. "Do you like them?"

Now that I know why she chose them, of course, I do. However, I'd prefer she wear nothing at all.

"Yes." My voice is barely a whisper. My need to possess her so great, my hearts pound in my chest. "You are beautiful, Holly."

She takes my hand and guides me down her body. I take great care to retract my claws so I do not accidentally scratch her.

She slips our joined hands beneath the scrap of silk between her thighs, and my heart hammers as she guides my fingers through her folds and I find them already slick. My nostrils flare as I scent her arousal.

"You are already ready for me?" I ask as I gently drag my finger through her warm, wet heat.

"You always make me feel like this," she admits.

My stav is hard and erect, extending from my mating pouch and throbbing with the need to join my body to hers. Her eyes widen when she feels the hard press of my length against her folds. The only thing separating us is the thin barrier of woven fabric.

She guides my thumb to the apex of her folds. She arches against my hand as I trace over the hooded flesh, and she moans, her face lighting with pleasure.

"Touch me here," she breathes.

I do as she asks, her hand guiding me until she is satisfied that I'm touching her just as she wishes. I love how she writhes beneath me and grows slicker with each passing moment.

She guides my mouth to her breast. "Kiss me here," she commands, and I obey.

Closing my mouth over the peak, I lave my tongue across the hard bead, scraping my fangs lightly across the sensitive flesh. She moans out my name, and I concentrate my attention on her other breast as well while still moving my hand through her folds.

She kneads the muscles of my shoulders and back before moving down my chest and abdomen, tracing the hard planes with her delicate fingers. When she reaches my stav, she wraps her hand around me, and I groan.

Her eyes widen slightly, and I look down to find her fingers do not quite meet. "You have ridges," she breathes against my mouth. "Just like your tongue."

"Is that bad?" I falter.

"No," she says. "It's just different from human men."

Worry expands in my chest. I know her people do not mate for life like mine do, but if she's had a mate before me, I am concerned that I may not live up to the standards he set. What if she is not pleased with the way I mate her?

She begins to lightly stroke my length, and I groan at the sensation. "You're so big, Rakan. I've never done this before, so we'll have to go slow until my body adjusts."

I cannot deny the pleasure that moves through me knowing that I will be the only male who ever touches her in this way. But I do not want to rush her.

I pull back and search her eyes. "We do not have to—"

She smiles. "I want to make love to you. I just… I've heard it can hurt the first time."

My hearts clench at the thought.

"I do not want to cause you pain, Holly. Let me please you instead." I move down her body and carefully pull the silken material down her legs, discarding it on the floor next to my bed. "May I taste you?"

Her mouth drifts open. "You want to do that?"

A low growl of arousal escapes me. "Yes."

She nods, and my gaze holds hers as I dip my head

between her thighs and drag my tongue through her wet heat.

A long moan escapes her, and her eyes roll to the back of her head.

The taste of her nectar is incredible. She is perfect, and she is mine. I concentrate my tongue around the hooded flesh she showed me when I first touched her. She writhes beneath my attentions, digging her heels into my shoulders as I taste and explore her. I band one arm over her hips to hold her in place.

She threads her hands through my hair as she begins to murmur a string of unintelligible words. Some of them sound Drakarian, but others, I suspect, are her native language.

Carefully, I insert one finger into her channel. She is so tight, my stav aches with the need to sheathe myself deep inside her. I long to feel her body as I stroke into her and fill her with my essence.

I grit my teeth as the mere thought of filling her with my seed drags me closer to the edge of my release. The tiny muscles of her core flex and quiver around my finger, then clamp down as she cries out my name.

Her form goes limp, and I move back up her body and capture her mouth with mine. She cups my cheek. "That was —there are no words, Rakan."

I smile, knowing that I have pleased her before I descend upon her lips again. "We are not done," I whisper against them.

As I curl my tongue around hers, I insert my finger again into her core. She moans into my mouth as I insert another and gently begin to pump them in and out like I long to do with my stav.

She grips my stav in her hand and strokes me in time

with the movement of my fingers. The friction is as exquisite as it is unbearable, and I worry that I will release too soon.

She clings tightly to me. "Rakan," she moans. "I want you."

I want her too, but I do not want to hurt her. "I will only pleasure you, my Holly," I whisper. "I refuse to hurt you."

She grips the back of my neck and pulls my lips back down to hers. "You're so wonderful," she whispers.

Her body tightens around me as I continue to pump my fingers into her while teasing my thumb over the small bundle of nerves that make her body light with pleasure.

She stills, then the muscles of her channel contract around my fingers while she strengthens her grip on my stav. As she finds her release, I find mine. I roar her name as my essence erupts from my stav and onto her abdomen, covering her with my seed.

She relaxes beneath me, and I remove my fingers from her channel then smooth my hand over her abdomen, spreading my essence across her petal-soft skin. I love that she is covered with my scent. She is mine, and I want every male to know this.

Her eyelids flutter as she smiles at me. I roll us both onto our sides, facing each other. I wrap my wings tightly around her and tug her close, pleased when she nestles into my warmth.

My stav is a hard bar between us, resting against her abdomen. She studies me for a moment, a question in her eyes. "You don't need time to recover?"

"Recover?"

"Your stav is still hard," she says. "I've heard human men need time to recover before they can make love again."

"Drakarians do not," I tell her.

I do not envy human men anything. They are small, weak, and now I discover they can only release once before they must recover. Perhaps they spend that time pleasuring their female until they can mate her again. Maybe that is why she is telling me this.

I touch her cheek. "Do you wish me to pleasure you more? I want only to please you, my Holly."

"You do please me, Rakan." She kisses me passionately. "That was incredible. I climaxed twice in one night."

Her tone implies twice is many times for her kind. I hope it is not, for when I fully mate her, I plan to take her repeatedly on our first night, and every night from then on if she will allow it.

I study her for a moment in concern. "Holly, I wish for us to see Healer Ranas."

She frowns. "Why?"

"I want him to make certain I will not hurt you during our first mating."

She kisses me again. "You are kind to worry about me, Rakan, but we don't have to do that. I know I'll be fine."

"How?"

"A little pain is normal for human women the first time we make love. We'll just have to go slow. All right?"

I wrap my wings around her, my concern lingering. "I will pleasure you every night in any way I can, my beautiful Holly, but I do not want to cause you any pain."

She smiles then crushes her lips to mine. "You are wonderful, you know that?"

Her words fill me with pride.

"We'll be fine if we go slow. I know we will."

I hope she is right. I cannot bear the thought of hurting her.

CHAPTER 25

HOLLY

As we lie in bed, I nestle into his chest. He tightens his arms and wings around me, and I've never felt so loved.

Now that we're together, he's going to stay. Relief floods my system. I could hardly bear the thought of him leaving for space.

I hate space. It's dangerous. Closing my eyes, I conjure an image of my father and shudder inwardly at the thought of anything happening to Rakan. I wouldn't be able to stand being stranded on Drakaria while I knew he was out in space, risking his life unnecessarily.

Now that we're together, we can start our life here.

When I wake in the morning, his head is between my thighs. He drags his tongue through my folds, and I moan as he teases the sensitive pearl at the top. When I come, it's with a keening cry.

He moves up my body before I've even come down from my climax and kisses me until I see stars. He inserts two fingers into my core and begins pumping them in and out. It doesn't take long for me to reach my climax again, and when I do, his *stav* pulses in my hand as he erupts onto my abdomen again, covering me with his essence.

We lounge in bed for a while, but once the morning light filters in through the window, I know we must get up.

He is Prince Varus's bodyguard. It's not as if he can take a day off.

He takes hold of my face and kisses me again. "We must get ready for our day. I will make you proud this day, my mate," he announces, and I smile. "I will win the Harvest Games. Tarok does not stand a chance against me."

My expression falls. "You still want to participate in the Harvest Games?"

Since we're together now, I expected him to withdraw so he can stay on Drakaria with me.

He grins. "Of course. It is a great honor, and I know that I will be victorious. Just watch. You will be proud of me."

I still don't understand. "I thought—"

He kisses me again, then stands from the bed. "Do not worry. I will beat Tarok swiftly. You will see, my Holly."

"This means... a lot to you, right?" I hedge, hoping beyond hope that he'll say no. That he'll change his mind about competing and decide to stay planetside.

"Of course. I have dreamed of such a day since I was a fledgling."

My heart sinks. He seems so excited. How can I ask him to just throw this opportunity away? What if it's been his dream to go to space? What if he resents me if I ask him to stay?

As all these questions run through my mind, I don't know how to voice them all. Or where to even begin.

He sits on the edge of the bed and leans down to give me another kiss. When he pulls back, he smiles. "I will watch for you in the stands."

I nod. "I'll be there cheering you on," I tell him with a half-hearted smile.

He moves to stand but then turns and kisses me once again. His red eyes are full of desire as they meet mine. A growl vibrates his chest as he cups my mons possessively. "I want to taste you again, my beautiful Holly."

Before I can respond, he drags me to the edge of the bed, kneels before me, and buries his face between my thighs. I moan and arch into his touch as he drags his tongue through my folds and a low purr vibrates his chest.

I thread my fingers through his hair and stare at the ceiling. Pleasure erupts so intensely that I come harder than I've ever come before.

He moves back up my body and kisses me deeply. His eyes pierce me, full of fierce possession.

I wrap my legs around his hips. "I want you."

He growls. "Do not tempt me. If I take you now, we will not leave this bed all day. When the games end and I am victorious, I will take you into the desert, and we will have a proper mating chase. I will claim you beneath the stars and the harvest moon this night, my Holly. You will scream my name to the night sky as I claim you, my beautiful mate."

His bold words leave me breathless and panting with longing. I want him now.

However, as he stands, he pulls me up with him. He hugs me close, wrapping his arms and wings tightly around me. His nostrils flare as he leans forward to skim the tip of his nose down the bridge of mine, then over to my temple down to my jaw. "You smell like me, my mate."

My mated friends have told me how important scent marking is to the Drakarians. When he presses a tender kiss to my neck, a shiver of pleasure moves through me. Tonight seems so very far away.

His eyes are full of promise as he pulls back.

I touch his cheek. "Rakan, why don't you just quit the games today? You don't have to continue, you know." I smirk. "We could start our mating chase now."

His gaze darkens with desire as his pupils expand until only a thin rim of red remains around the edges.

A sharp knock at the door startles us abruptly. He sobers and turns toward the door. "Yes?"

"Prince Varus is seeking you. It is time to report for the games."

He turns back to me. "I must go."

I press a tender kiss to his lips. "I'm sure Varus will understand if you—"

He sighs heavily. "Quitting the games now would be dishonorable." He takes my hand and places it over his hearts. "You are mine. My fated one. I know that once I prove myself to you, the fated mark will appear."

The fate mark—how could I have forgotten about it? I peer at his chest. "Can you feel that I'm... yours in that way?"

He nods. "I know it deep in my hearts."

"What if I'm not?"

"You are meant to be mine, just as I am meant to be yours," he insists. "Once I prove myself to you, you will see for yourself."

My brow furrows. "Is that why you're participating? To prove to me that we should be together?"

He nods. "I failed you once, Holly. I do this to prove my worth to you. To show you that I am worthy to be your mate. That I—"

"Rakan!" Someone else pounds on the door. "The prince awaits."

He gives my cheek a quick peck. "I must go. I will seek you out after I win."

∼

As I take my seat next to Anna in the stands, she turns and tackles me in a bear hug. "I'm so happy for you. I just knew you two would end up together."

"Thanks." I grin. "But... how did you know?"

Lilly laughs. "Rakan's room is next to ours, and you left the balcony door open."

My jaw drops, and my cheeks heat in embarrassment. "Oh, my gosh. I had no idea!"

"It's all right. Varus and I are loud sometimes, too."

"Sometimes?" Anna arches a brow.

Lilly chuckles.

Prince Kaj inclines his head. "I am certain Rakan will be an excellent mate to you and a wonderful father to your fledglings. He is an honorable male."

"Thank you." I smile, trying to remain cheerful, but my consternation must bleed through because Anna takes my hand.

"Is something wrong?"

"It's just... if he wins, he'll be among the warriors chosen to go into space."

Prince Kaj's brow furrows. "Surely he will not leave now that he has a mate?"

I shrug. "We're not officially mated yet. I... don't want to ask him to sacrifice his dream just for me. These games are important to him. He says it's a great honor to compete and an even greater one to win."

Prince Kaj darts a glance around us. "Where is Varus?"

Lilly motions to the arena. "He's competing, too." She laughs. "He says he wants to impress me with his skills."

Kaj purses his lips. "Of course, he would wish to show off to his mate." He stands. "I must find him and speak to him."

Without another word, he leaves.

CHAPTER 26

RAKAN

As I wait in the training area for the games to begin, I can hardly wait to see the expression on Holly's face when I win. She will burst with pride to be mated to such an honorable male.

I look off to the side and see Tal—personal guard to King Raidyn of the Wind Clan. He walks over to me. "I have heard a rumor you do this to impress a human female. Is this truth?"

I study him a moment. It was not long ago that we were enemies. I am glad, however, that those days are gone now. "Yes. Why do you ask?"

His ice blue eyes study me, and I note that his dark gray scales are buffed to a fine sheen. I arch a brow. "Are you trying to impress a human female as well?"

He sighs heavily. "Yes. The one named Aria." He darts a glance at his chest, placing his hand directly over his hearts. "I feel that she is mine, but my mark has yet to appear."

"Have you spoken with her? Does she feel the same?"

Tal shakes his head. "She is afraid of me and my kin because of the attack led by my people on the city not long ago."

I pity him. Many of the human females do not trust the Wind Clan because of this. I know that Tal was not among those who attacked. In fact, he helped us to fight off the ones who did.

"Give them time," I tell him. "When we gather in your territory for the Wind Clan Harvest Games, the humans will see that not all of you were to blame. And that there are honorable males among your warriors."

He nods. "I hope you are right, my friend." He claps a hand on my shoulder. "Good luck in the games and with your female."

"Thank you."

Tal walks away and Prince Varus walks over to me. "I am truly happy for you, Rakan. But are you certain you still wish to compete?"

I still. "What do you mean?"

He regards me curiously. "If you win, you will go into space. You will not see Holly for many turns of the moon."

My expression falls. I had not considered this. I'd been so intent upon proving myself to her that I failed to realize once I did, I would be separated from her for long periods. I... do not want this.

I meet his gaze. "I must prove myself to her. This is the best way to do so."

He arches a brow. "Is it?"

I open my mouth to ask him what he means, but Prince Kaj interrupts, pulling his attention away from me.

I walk away, giving them their privacy, and notice Tarok practicing defensive maneuvers in the far corner.

I tip up my chin with a teasing smirk. "You do not stand a chance against me, you know."

Tarok laughs. "Oh, I have no doubt that I'll win this day. I just want to do it fairly, that's all."

My brow furrows. "What do you mean?"

"Have you talked to your Holly about these games?"

"Of course, I have."

He pins me with a pointed stare. "What does she think about you going into space once you win?"

I blink. He is the second male to point this out to me. How is it that everyone else has considered this, but I have not?

The answer occurs to me instantly. I have been so focused on winning over Holly that I've been oblivious to all other concerns.

It is unlike me not to plan several steps ahead. Every good warrior practices foresight, and yet... I failed on this occasion, it seems.

"Rakan?" Prince Varus calls. "I'd like to speak with you again."

I excuse myself from my conversation with Tarok and join Varus. His timing is fortunate, for I have something I must share.

I plan to withdraw from the event; I cannot allow myself to compete and potentially win. Not when victory means that I will be separated from my Holly.

Varus looks to me. "I understand you are now with Holly."

"Yes. That is why I must withdraw from the games. I do not wish to leave her behind if I win."

Varus smiles. "You do not have to. It has been decided that the winner may choose to gift their prize to the person they defeat in the final round of the games."

Relief fills me. "This is excellent news."

The Prince smiles. "Now. Let us ready ourselves to compete."

He walk to the other side of the room and begins practicing his defensive moves.

CHAPTER 27

HOLLY

Carefully, I step down to the training area. On the speakers overhead, I can hear Prince Varus announcing the start of the games. I just hope I arrive before they begin.

As soon as I enter the training area, I spot my target. Tarok is in the far corner, practicing his moves. Across the room, I notice my beloved Rakan. He's sitting on one of the benches, facing away from us.

I duck behind a column and hiss, "Tarok?"

He stills and glances around, trying to locate the source of the sound.

"Over here." I step out from behind the column just enough for him to spot me.

He grins. "I've been expecting you."

"You have?"

"Yes." He gestures to Rakan. "Your mate is over there."

I shake my head. "I didn't come to see him. I came to see you."

He frowns. "I… do not understand."

"I need you to win the games."

His head jerks back. "What?"

"Whatever happens, I need you to beat Rakan. I'm begging you. You can't let him win."

Awareness pricks the back of my neck and startles me. I turn to find Rakan standing behind me, betrayal etched into his features.

"You came here to ask another male—no," he corrects, "to *beg* another male to beat me in the games?" He shakes his head. "Why would you do this?"

"Rakan, let me explain."

His eyes widen as they shift to Tarok then back to me. "You have changed your mind. You want Tarok as your mate instead."

He seems so devastated, I rush toward him, but he flinches away.

"Rakan, that's not—"

"No. You do not need to console me. I am strong, and I… will not stand in your way if this is what you want."

"It's not what I want."

"I just overheard you asking him to beat me. What kind of mate begs another to defeat their beloved?"

"You don't understand, Rakan. I—"

"Do not worry. I will not harm him beyond what can be repaired by the Healers. I would not harm the male you chose," he grinds out, then levels an icy glare at Tarok." And you! I *will* defeat you. You do not stand a chance."

Before I can interject, he whirls around and rushes away with inhuman Drakarian speed.

Tarok sighs heavily and arches a brow. "I am going to suffer this day—more than I already expected to. I just know it. The two of you ought to name your first fledgling after me for all the pain I am about to endure."

"I—"

He laughs. "Thank goodness Healer Ranas is here. I expect I will be close to death by the time your mate is done with me."

My jaw drops. How can he joke at a moment like this?

Having noticed the despair in my expression, he places a hand on my shoulder and meets my gaze. "Do not worry. I merely jest. All will be well. You will see."

CHAPTER 28

HOLLY

I trudge back to the stands, and Lilly leans over to me. "Did you speak with him?"

"Yes, but it… didn't exactly go as planned."

She frowns. "What do you mean?"

"Rakan now thinks I want Tarok instead of him because I asked Tarok to beat him in the games."

"Why didn't you just consult Rakan directly and ask him to throw the fight?"

"I already know he won't. He's all about honor, so… I don't think he could pretend to lose."

She combs a stray lock of hair behind my ear. "All is not lost. You can talk to him after the games and explain why you asked Tarok to beat him. I'm sure he'll understand, Holly."

I nod and drop into my chair. I hope she's right.

Tarok enters the arena and everyone cheers. The applause grows deafening when Rakan strides out after him, and the announcer proclaims they will face off.

They shift into draka form, and my jaw drops. I don't

think I'll ever get used to how enormous these shifters are, and how much they resemble the mythical dragons of Earth.

Rakan's orange-red scales gleam beneath the sun. His long, tapered tail lashes back and forth behind him in irritation as he glares at Tarok, his red eyes burning with anger. Tall black horns spiral from his massive head, and he bares fangs the length of my forearm as he snarls at Tarok.

It's hard to watch them circle one another for a moment before they attack. Each swipes and kicks ruthlessly at the other. Rakan moves with a deadly, fluid grace, his movements precise and measured, while Tarok is more unpredictable in his actions.

They appear to be evenly matched, however. I note how Tarok struggles to push back as Rakan rushes toward him when he stumbles. Rakan's expression is full of betrayal when he glances up into the stands and his eyes meet mine.

They roll on the ground in a tangled mesh of claws and fangs before splitting apart and rushing each other again. They take to the air, spiraling in freefall as they tear at each other.

I gasp, anxious for their safety as obsidian blood rains onto the arena.

The Drakarian crowd watches nonchalantly, but all of us humans exclaim in dread and fear that someone will be killed at any moment. I can hardly stand how strikingly violent these games are.

I jump up from my chair. "Stop!"

Rakan and Tarok pull apart, and their heads whip toward me.

CHAPTER 29

RAKAN

I gaze down at my Holly, who looks devastated.

"Please, Rakan," she begs. "I don't want you to do this. You'll get hurt."

"I am fine," I reply.

"I am, as well," Tarok answers.

She shakes her head. "And if you win, then what?" she cries, the crowd's attention fixed on her. "Then you'll just leave me to roam around space for months at a time?"

I blink, stupefied. Prince Varus said the prize could be gifted to another.

"I asked you before to stay with me," she says. "Do you remember what you said?"

My mind returns to the day she lay injured in the Med Center. I held her hand, and she squeezed mine gently as her eyes met mine.

"Please," she whispered. "Will you stay with me?"

"Always," I had answered.

I turn to Tarok, and he dips his chin in acknowledgment.

I realize now that he knew this is how our fight would end all along. That's why he predicted he would beat me.

I realize now that Holly wants me to prove that I choose her over everything else... even over the honor of winning the Harvest Games.

I glance once more at my beautiful mate. *This,* I will do for her gladly.

Tarok and I land and circle each other. I put on a great show of fighting, but my heart is no longer in the game. Still, I will leave no room for any to question his honor.

When Tarok pins me to the ground, my performance is so believable that Holly rushes into the arena and throws herself upon me as he's declared the winner. The crowd roars its approval as Varus awards Tarok the champion's medal.

She cups my cheek, her eyes staring deep into mine, full of worry. "How badly are you hurt?"

A slow grin curves my mouth as I gaze at Holly. "I am better now that you are here, my Holly."

Instantly, I shift forms and pull her into my arms, pressing a series of tender kisses all over her cheeks, nose, and brow.

She laughs, shoves my chest playfully, and narrows her eyes at me. "You threw the match for me, didn't you?"

I arch a teasing brow. "I do not know what you mean. Tarok is by far the superior warrior."

She laughs and then falls into my arms as I kiss her.

A soft glow draws my attention, and I glance down at my chest to find the fated mark swirling across my scales. Her eyes drop to the spot as well, and she smiles. "You were right. We *are* meant to be together."

She embraces me as I struggle to suppress a growl of arousal. "Do you choose me, Holly?"

"Yes."

"Good," I rasp as desire burns through my veins like fire. "Because I have chosen you."

Without warning, I gather her into my arms and lift her into the sky.

She lets out a surprised yelp as we swoop over the city and proceed toward the great crimson desert beyond.

I promised my mate a proper mating chase, and she will have one.

Gently, I lower her to the sands in a space surrounded by boulders and towers of rock. She will need many places to hide so I may chase her.

I shift into draka form. "Give yourself to me," I growl.

A smile crests her lips. "No."

She turns to flee as tradition dictates. Since she is human and slower than me, I give her a head start, though I can hardly stand still because I want her so badly. Need roars through me.

CHAPTER 30

HOLLY

I sprint away and hide behind a group of boulders. Goosebumps prickle my flesh as a low, predatory growl rumbles nearby. The scent of spice and cinnamon surrounds me, and I know the dragon is close. Rakan is a predator, and I am his prey, but I will not be taken easily.

Fear and arousal spike through me as warm breath skates across the back of my neck, parting my long, blonde hair.

"I can scent your need, my mate," he purrs.

I still. My nipples prick against the front of my dress, and my pulse pounds between my thighs. He's so close, the delicious warmth of his body radiates to mine. The rough vibrations of his chest move through me, and heat pools deep in my core.

For a moment, I'm unable to move, paralyzed by my intense desire. Shivers of pleasure and fear move down my spine as my body hums in awareness of him.

"Give yourself to me," he demands, his voice deep and husky.

My heart hammers in anticipation as I lick my dry lips. Slowly, I spin to face him. The sunlight glints off his orange-red scales. His lethal dark claws score the sand as he advances, a predator closing in on his prey. I inhale sharply when he bares his teeth, revealing two large rows of sharp, menacing fangs.

"Give yourself to me, my beautiful Holly."

He flicks his long, tapered tail as he lowers his massive, horned head. His reptilian, red-rimmed pupils contract and expand. His nostrils flare, drawing in my scent before he releases a quick huff of air, nearly knocking me over.

"Give yourself to me." A menacing snarl rises from his chest. "Now."

Dust and wind suddenly swirl around me, and I squeeze my eyes shut against the fine grains of sand.

When I open them, Rakan stands before me in his two-legged form. My gaze travels over his body. I lick my lips again in anticipation as my eyes travel over the hard planes of muscle that cover him from head to toe, imagining him moving between my thighs.

A pair of twisted, onyx horns frame his long, red-orange hair, drawing my attention to his face. His eyes are full of hunger.

His long, tapered tail wraps around my leg and snakes up my thigh. My gaze travels down his body, and I'm transfixed as his long, thick shaft emerges from the slit between his legs.

My thighs involuntarily squeeze together while I allow my eyes to roam over the ridges lining his fully engorged, erect length, imagining how it will feel inside me. Liquid beads on the tip before spilling over and dripping onto the sand.

He steps forward and reaches out to cup my breast

through the fabric of my dress. A soft moan escapes me when he brushes his thumb over the already stiff peak, careful to keep his lethal, black claws retracted.

"Give yourself to me," he rasps, his gaze darkened by hunger. "I long to fill you with my seed and claim you as mine."

Cautiously, I touch the tip of his length. A sharp hiss escapes his gritted teeth as his red eyes grow increasingly fiery and possessive. Desire ripples through me. I cannot deny the urge to surrender, but I will not allow myself to be conquered so easily.

I want to give him the chase he would expect from a Drakarian woman.

I push his hand away from my body, but he grabs my wrist and pulls me closer, growling. Instead of terror, I feel arousal at the sheer power of his massive body pressing against mine. My nipples are hard against his silken scales as he drags me against his chest. His erection is a hard bar against my abdomen. Another bead of liquid escapes the tip and seeps through the fabric of my dress.

With one arm banded around my waist, holding me flush against him, he trails his other hand down the length of my body, his lethal claws slicing a line down the fabric of my dress and revealing my bare flesh to his touch. His gaze never wavers as he fists the delicate, satin fabric between my thighs in one hand. I gasp when he rips the underwear from my body.

He drags his fingers through my already slick folds. A desperate moan escapes my mouth when he touches the small bundle of nerves at the top. He lifts his hand away and brings his fingers to his lips, tasting me. His eyes roll to the back of his head as if he relishes my taste. A pleased purr sounds in his chest, and his eyes snap open.

"Give yourself to me," he demands.

CHAPTER 31

RAKAN

Her blue eyes sear me. She wants me as much as I desire her. I can scent her need on the wind. My mate may be human, but she is as stubborn as a Drakarian female. The mating chase is an ancient practice, and she understands it well.

She will not be conquered easily, my female. She will make me work to claim her.

The muscles ripple beneath my scales in anticipation of claiming her. Now, I need only to convince her to give herself to me.

Her taste is exquisite. The delicious nectar of her core lingers on my tongue, and I long for more. Her gaze holds mine as I grip the silken strands of her long blonde hair between my fingers and tip her head back, exposing the elegant column of her neck.

Her chest rises and falls rapidly as she waits for my next move. I tear off her robe, baring her petal-soft skin to my gaze. I dip my head to the curve of her collar, flaring my nostrils to draw her intoxicating scent deep into my lungs.

I trail a line of kisses to the valley of her breasts, darting my tongue out to taste the sweet salt of her skin. I lave my tongue across one stiff peak then close my mouth over the tender flesh. She gasps and runs her fingers through my hair, pulling me even closer.

The scent of her need grows stronger with each passing moment, suffusing the air, threatening to overwhelm and consume me.

"You are mine," I growl. "Give yourself to me."

My control hangs by barely a thread as I gently bear her to the ground. Her eyes are half-lidded and heated as I settle between her thighs.

She is a beautiful, ethereal creature beneath the soft light of the harvest moon that rises behind us.

This female is mine, and I intend to claim her and bind her to me in all ways according to the ancient rituals of my people.

I long to taste her on my tongue yet again. I wrap my tail around her thigh, opening her further. Clenching my jaw, I struggle to hold onto my control as I study my mate.

"Beautiful," I whisper. "You are perfect."

I long to bury myself inside her, to fill her with my seed until she can hold no more. I want every male that comes near to scent that she is mine and mine alone. I will take her many times tonight, but first, I must convince her to surrender.

Her pupils are wide, and her beautiful skin is flushed with arousal. My feral gaze, full of need, reflects in her luminous blue eyes as I cover her smaller form with my body. She inhales sharply when the hard length of my stav presses against her inner thigh.

"Do you feel how much I desire you, my mate? Give yourself to me," I whisper in her ear. I clench my jaw, struggling to maintain my control as the crown of my stav strains against her entrance. "I will claim you beneath the stars so that every male in Drakaria will know you belong only to me."

A short puff of air escapes her, and she trembles as I run my hand down the length of her body. As much as I long to sheathe myself inside her, I want to pleasure her first.

I hold her gaze as I shift my weight back then gently guide her legs over my shoulders. I dip my head between her thighs and run my tongue through her slick folds. As soon as I touch the small bundle of nerves at the top, she moans and arches into me.

She digs her heels into my back and her fingers into my hair to hold me in place. I love all the mewls of pleasure she makes as I tease my tongue over her sensitive flesh. Slowly, I insert one finger into the entrance of her core. The small muscles of her channel contract around me.

"More!" She wraps her hands around my horns, tugging insistently. I love when she demands that I please her.

The last of my tightly wound control begins to slip as I concentrate my attention on the small pearl of flesh that makes her light with pleasure. Her body goes taut for a moment before she cries out my name, flooding my tongue with the sweet taste of her nectar.

Satisfied that I've made her scream my name to the stars, I lift my head to study her expectantly. My body aches with need, and my stav twitches in anticipation of sheathing deep in her wet heat. I long to claim her completely.

I move up her body and stroke her face.

"Give yourself to me," I groan. "Take me inside you, and I will give you my seed as I claim you beneath the harvest moon."

CHAPTER 32

HOLLY

I'm panting heavily, and I haven't even come down from my climax before he moves up my body and touches my face. "Give yourself to me. Take me inside you and I will give you my seed as I claim you beneath the harvest moon."

His tail snakes around my ankle. Panting heavily, he stares down at me, the silver moonlight accentuating the hard planes of muscle that define his abdomen and chest. My gaze travels down his form to his still fully erect *stav*.

"I want you," I whisper, breathless with anticipation.

He growls. "I will take you many times this night, my mate."

A soft moan escapes me at his words as my heart continues to pound frantically.

He drops so that his massive body covers mine and pins me beneath him. The vibrations of his chest and the pounding of his dual hearts against my chest make my stomach flutter. Heat floods my channel as he dips his head to the curve of my neck and shoulder, skimming the tip of his nose along my sensitive skin. A vibrating purr escapes him as he inhales deeply.

"Say the words," he whispers as he begins to tease his thumb over the sensitive pearl of flesh between my thighs. "Tell me you are mine."

"I'm yours." I murmur. "I am your mate."

His tail wraps around my thigh, opening my legs so he can settle between them. His expression softens and he cups my cheek. "You are certain you want me, my Holly?"

I smile against his lips. "Yes."

He kisses me long and deep and then fits the tip of his *stav* at my entrance. My body aches with need; I long to take him inside me. His pupils are blown so wide that only a thin rim of red is visible around the edges.

"Mine," he growls.

The crown of his *stav* pushes into my entrance, and I inhale sharply. The breath stutters from my lungs as he slowly enters me. The delicious stretch deep inside my channel as he fills me completely makes my toes curl with pleasure.

An intense burst of heat suffuses my core, and I arch against him, nearly coming right then from the intense pleasure. "What was that?" I barely manage.

"My precum to soften your womb," he breathes.

He rocks his hips back and forth until he is fully seated inside me. He smooths a hand down my body and cups my breast. A soft moan escapes my lips as he teases the hard, beaded tip between his thumb and forefinger.

I arch against him, wanting more, and he releases a tortured groan.

"So tight," he rasps as he begins shallow thrusts into my

channel, the ridges of his *stav* creating the most delicious friction.

"Forgive me, my *linaya*," he groans. "My need is too great."

Heat coils tightly in my core at his words. Each thrust deepens as his pace increases. I trace my fingers down the length of his spine, feeling the flex of his muscles as he strokes deep inside me.

He drops down low, wrapping his arms up under my back as he holds me close, his hearts beating in his chest against mine. I tighten my legs around him and a deep growl escapes him, the vibrations of it moving through my entire body.

Pleasure builds inside me and I'm so close, the small muscles of my channel begin to quiver and flex around his length.

He groans and another heated burst of his precum hits my womb. The warmth ignites inside me, tipping me over the edge. My release rushes through my body. I throw my head back and cry out his name as wave after wave of pleasure ripples through me.

His *stav* begins to pulse. "Mine," he roars as he erupts deep in my channel, filling me with his seed. He holds me tightly against his chest, his form trembling as he wraps his hand around my hip in an almost bruising grip as he continues to come. It triggers another orgasm within me, this one stronger than the last.

Panting heavily as I come down from my pleasure, I stroke his cheek. "I love you, Rakan."

His *stav* is still buried deep inside me, hard and erect. He presses a series of kisses from my temple down my jaw to the curve of my neck and shoulder as he cups one breast. My nipple stiffens again beneath his attentions while he begins to move once more.

"I love you too, my beautiful Linaya."

I run my fingers through his shoulder-length, flame-red hair and pull his mouth back down to mine in a passionate kiss as he begins to stroke deep inside me. "I must have you again, my beautiful Holly."

A soft moan escapes me at his words as I wrap myself tightly around him. "I'm yours, my love."

EPILOGUE

Holly

I smile as I watch Rakan fly overhead. His wings billow at his sides like great sails as he carefully lowers himself to the ground.

He moves toward me and gathers me into his arms. He lifts my feet off the ground and spins me around as he captures my mouth in a passionate kiss. My abdomen is slightly rounded with our child, but Rakan is strong enough to hold me without issue.

The children gather around us, interrupting our tender moment. He smiles brightly at them as he sets me back on my feet. "What did Miss Holly teach you this day?"

"She was teaching us our letters," one of my students exclaims.

"Please, Rakan, will you show us how to fight?"

He laughs and crouches low as if readying to attack them.

They shriek with laughter and flee, and he pretends to chase after them.

I watch with my hand resting protectively on my

abdomen. I can hardly wait to see him playing with our child. He's going to be an amazing father.

He rushes back to me and sweeps me into his arms again as he places a series of kisses across my cheeks, nose, and brow. I laugh and playfully push him away before he captures my mouth in a claiming kiss.

I glance over his shoulder. "What happened to the children?"

He arches a brow. "I told them to go play hide and seek."

"You aren't even trying to find them."

"Yet," he corrects. "*First*, I will lavish attention on my mate. *Then*, I will seek them out."

I dissolve into laughter while he settles me into his lap. I lean against him and gaze up at the sky. "I'm so glad you aren't up there, searching the stars."

He sighs. "Me too. I only hope that Tarok is happy, wherever he is."

I place a hand on his chest, directly over the swirling fate mark.

"I pray that he finds what we have, my love. I wish everyone could be as happy as we are."

He splays his palm over my abdomen, his gorgeous red gaze never leaving mine. "I thought for so long that I had failed you. When you were injured during the Wind Clan attack, I thought you would never want to be my mate"

I touch his face. "You never failed me, Rakan. You saved me."

He drops his forehead gently to mine. "Thank you for choosing me, Holly."

"I didn't choose you." I run the soft pad of my thumb across his cheek as I stare deep into his eyes. "We chose each other, my love."

"I am yours, and you are mine," he whispers against my lips. "Always, my Linaya."

ABOUT ARIA WINTER

Thank you so much for reading this. I hope you enjoyed this story. If you enjoyed this book, please leave a review on Amazon (Click Here) and/or Goodreads. I would really appreciate it. Reviews are the lifeblood of Indie Authors.

The next book in the Elemental Dragon Warrior series is available here: Saved By The Wind Dragon Guard

For information about upcoming releases Like me on Facebook (www.facebook.com/ariawinterauthor) or sign up for upcoming release alerts at my website:

Ariawinter.com

Want more?
Elemental Dragon Warriors Series

Claimed by the Fire Dragon Prince
Stolen by the Wind Dragon Prince
Rescued by the Water Dragon Prince
Healed by the Earth Dragon Prince
Chosen By The Fire Dragon Guard
Saved By The Wind Dragon Guard
Treasured By The Water Dragon Guard
Taken By The Earth Dragon Guard

Want more Dragon Shifters? Check out my Beauty and the Beast Retelling below.
Once Upon A Fairy Tale Romance Series

Taken by the Dragon: A Beauty and the Beast Retelling
Captivated by the Fae: A Cinderella Retelling
Rescued By The Merman: A Little Mermaid Retelling
Bound to the Elf Prince: A Snow White Retelling

Cosmic Guardian Series

Charmed by the Fox's Heart
Seduced by the Peacock's Beauty
Protected by the Spider's Web
Ensnared by the Serpent's Gaze
Forged by the Dragon's Flame

Once Upon a Shifter Series
Ella and her Shifters
Snow White And Her Werewolves

ABOUT JADE WALTZ

Jade Waltz lives in Illinois with her husband, two sons, and her three crazy cats. She loves knitting, playing video games, and watching Esports. Jade's passions include the arts, green tea and mints — all while writing and teaching marching band drill in the fall.

Jade has always been an avid reader of the fantasy, paranormal and sci-fi genres and wanted to create worlds she always wanted to read.

She writes character driven romances within detailed universes, where happily-ever-afters happen for those who dare love the abnormal and the unknown. Their love may not be easy—but it is well worth it in the end.

Thank you for taking the time to read my book!
    Please take a moment to leave a review! <3
    Reviews are important for indie self-publishing authors and they help us grow.

Connect with me at:

Facebook Author Page: Jade Waltz
    Facebook Group: Jade Waltz Literary Alcove
    Twitter: @authorjadewaltz
    Instagram: @authorjadewaltz

Email: authorjadewaltz@gmail.com

Sign up for my newsletter:
Jade Waltz Newsletter
No Spam! I Promise! <3

Other Works Found At:
Website: www.jadewaltz.com
Amazon Profile: Jade Waltz
Bookbub: Jade Waltz

Project Universe Links:

Found
Achieve
Develop

Bird of Prey
Scaled Heart

Failure

Project: Adapt
    Found

A failed human prototype. That's all she is…

Born and raised as an experiment, Selena's life has been filled with torture, betrayal, and distrust… but one night changes everything.

Sold, attacked, and on the run, Selena is picked up by a colony ship. Struggling to find her place on this ship and trying to understand the draw she feels toward two alien males, her already uncertain life becomes downright unimaginable when she learns new life is growing inside her.

Terrified her captors will find her and take her and her children back to a life of horror and captivity, she must learn to trust her saviors, and herself.

With the help of her two mates, Selena will fight for her freedom—or die trying.

Found is the first book in a space fantasy alien romance series which will have the heroine travel through the galaxy, experiencing new things and meeting multiple aliens along the way.

Order NOW!

Other Series Cowritten w/ Aria Winter:

Elemental Dragon Warriors - Alien/Dragon Shifter Romance - MF
Claimed by the Fire Dragon Prince
We set out from Earth in search of a new world. I never thought it would end with us crashing on a planet full of dragon shifters.

When I'm taken from my people by a fierce Drakarian warrior, my first thought is of escape. Varus is the Prince of the Fire Clan. He claims the glowing pattern on his chest means that I'm his fated one—his Linaya.

I doubt he's going to just let me go. But what does it mean to be fated to a dragon?
Read Now!